A Brooke and Daniel Psychological Thriller

DELIRIUM

J.F.PENN

This book is a work of fiction. The characters, incidents and dialogue are drawn from the author's imagination and are not to be construed as real. Any resemblance to actual events or persons, living or dead, is fictionalized or coincidental.

Cover and Interior Design: JD Smith Design

Printed by Lightning Source Ltd

CURL UP
PRESS

www.CurlUpPress.com

For Jonathan, who accepts the crazy in me.

And for my readers, for whom I put these dark thoughts on the page.

"Those who the Gods wish to destroy,
they first make mad."

Anonymous ancient proverb

"He punishes the children for the sin of the parents
to the third and fourth generation."

Numbers 14:18

PROLOGUE

"Here we see the mad as monstrosities and tainted creatures."

Dr Christian Monro advanced the slide to show a vintage black and white picture: a man huddled in a corner with haunted eyes, his dirty straitjacket mottled with blood. "We must, of course, treat such as these with humanity but we must also ensure their stain does not continue into the next generation." Christian paused, savoring the moment of complete attention. "The implementation of my proposals will safeguard the future of our great nation. Thank you."

Applause filled the small room, and Christian bowed his head a little, acknowledging their respect. He had been courting this group for years now, the politicians and the religious right, as well as those in big business who funded the enterprise. He breathed in deeply, a smile playing over his lips. Finally, they were taking his work seriously, which was surely worth the sacrifice of those he had referred to the research centers.

Christian pushed the faint glimmer of guilt down as the applause ended and one of the more senior figures in the room nodded slowly at him, a promise of future favor in his gaze. Dr Damian Crowther was bald, his head angular and smooth, with one eye blue and the other brown. Despite his distinctive appearance, Crowther wasn't a man anyone stared at for long. Christian had heard rumors of the doctor's investigations into the farthest reaches of the mind, where madness bled into what some would call the paranormal. Crowther's favor was known to be a double-edged sword, but perhaps it was time to embrace the risks for the potential of a higher reward.

As Crowther turned away, Christian looked at his watch, worry gnawing at the edges of his triumph. He didn't want to rush away, but he had to make the meeting and none of these men could know about it.

After extricating himself from the late-night whiskey drinking, Christian grabbed a taxi to South London, patting his top pocket where he had the money in a cream envelope. It was a small price to pay for breathing space, but once he had power behind him, Christian would deal with the blackmailer. Handing them over for research purposes would make for appropriate recompense.

The Imperial War Museum was lit from below, a spectacular edifice, a symbol of Britain's military might. Of course, Christian had visited before, but it had been more out of curiosity for the building's past. The Bethlem Hospital had once been based here, the original Bedlam of nightmare, where the groans of the suffering were muted by thick walls. The note had told him to go around to the side gate, so Christian walked around the perimeter. It was open as promised and he walked through, into the trees at the side of the expansive park space. He strode towards the side door, gathering his confidence as a suit of armor, made stronger by his earlier triumph. Perhaps he would give this blackmailer a talking to instead. He flexed his fingers … maybe something more than that.

The inside of the building was dark, with just a few floor lights leading inward. Christian could hear faint sounds of music down the corridor, a mournful violin, the deep notes of a cello. A door was ajar further into the museum. He walked to it and stepped inside, apprehension overtaken by curiosity.

Candles burned in the corners of the room and shadows flickered on the walls. In the dim light, Christian saw a large wooden object and he stepped further into the room to see it more clearly. A sudden movement of air and a shift of shadows made his eyes narrow. He turned, but it was too late. A needle jabbed his neck and Christian raised his hand to the wound, suddenly dizzy. He sank to the floor, suddenly faint. There was someone else here with him, but the figure retreated quickly back to the gloom, out of his reach.

"What … have you done?" Christian murmured, as his throat tightened and weakness deadened his limbs. "I have your money."

"Money you received for betraying those who trusted you," the whisper came in the dark. "I don't want it. But I do want you to remember before you die, for what you have done is just a reflection of what your ancestors once did in this place."

Colors appeared in front of Christian's eyes, morphing into the shapes of creatures that landed on the walls around him. They had tiny needle-like teeth and he tried to move away from them, but their legs scuttled fast as they swarmed onto him and he had no strength to bat them away. His skin itched but Christian couldn't raise his arms to scratch. His heart thudded in his chest. It was a drug – some kind of hallucinogen. It had to be, but knowing didn't change how he felt. Biting, tearing, tiny knives slashing a thousand cuts across his flesh as the creatures began to feast.

"Please," Christian panted, heart racing, breath ragged. "What do you want?"

The figure came out of the shadows, like a nightmare from history, an echo of the photo Christian had shown earlier that night. The man wore a dirty straitjacket, stained with blood and pus. The arms hung loose, long sleeves dragging on the floor, the straps hanging down. A black mask covered his eyes and nose, and Christian could see that the man's dark eyes were bright with intent. There was no madness within.

"You call them monstrosities, tainted blood that must be bred out. But it is you who are defective, a blemish to be erased. And now you're in here, you must be crazy. Welcome to the lunatics' ball, Monro."

The man threw his hands in the air and spun in place, the ties from the straitjacket whirling about him, creating a vortex that Christian couldn't tear his eyes from. The string instruments soared, filling the room with a cacophony of jarring noise, grating against his brain. Christian was transfixed by the whirling, as the colors shattered and the fuzzy feeling intensified. It seemed that other figures joined the man as the music played on, shadows turning into the phantoms of those who had been locked up here so long ago. A beautiful girl with bare feet whirled in place, spinning around, her thin arms held like a ballerina. She opened her mouth to smile and Christian saw that her teeth were all missing, her gums bloody emptiness – a victim of force-feeding. A hulking figure appeared next to her, his head bound with bandages around a broken jaw, moaning in a grotesque parody of joy as he lumbered to the center of the room to turn with them. Another man dragged himself across the floor towards Christian, his head shaved, electrodes still attached, drool dripping down his chin. His eyes locked on the doctor, but his stare was fixed, as if no soul dwelled behind that facade of humanity.

Christian tried to push himself up and away from the wall, but the man in the straitjacket bore down upon him. The figures in the room dissipated and floated away as his image alone sharpened into focus once again. Had there even been any others? Christian knew the drug had a deep hold now, his mind tilted by chemical intrusion. He had no strength to fight as the man dragged him across the floor.

"Perhaps you're feeling a little stressed?" the man spat, his words bitter as he hoisted Christian onto the wooden chair, buckling straps at his ankles and wrists. Christian struggled, but it was as if he was in a thick soup and his limbs wouldn't obey his brain's command. The man bent down and picked up a padded wooden box with straps to hold the two sides together. "This should help."

Christian tried to shout, to scream, but the drugs had deadened his tongue and made it thick like a lump of liver. He could only moan as the man placed the box over his head and tightened the straps. It was heavy and dense, the darkness absolute. Christian's heart thumped in his chest as he tried to breathe through his nose, but the box was tight against his skull with only a small hole for air. He was on the edge of consciousness, panic rising as his heart rate spiraled out of control. He felt a knock against the box on top of his head and the noise of a flap being opened. A chink of light enabled Christian to see the padding inside, a dull off-white, the color of old sheets, right in front of his eyes. Then, he felt a drip of cold water on the top of his skull.

He shook his head violently, rattling the restraints that held his arms and legs. But he couldn't move far enough away and the water kept dripping, faster now. It became a thin stream that pooled under his chin, rising in cold inches against his skin. Christian closed his mouth as the level rose to his lips. He tipped his head, angling it to allow him breathing space, but he only succeeded in trickling water up his nose. Christian spluttered, trying to breathe and cough, but the water kept coming.

He heard laughter against the backdrop of music, and he imagined the spinning figures watching his torture, their eyes shining in anticipation of his end. Christian jerked and writhed, fighting to escape the stream. He moaned as panic overwhelmed him. The water level was almost at his nose now, covering his mouth. He threw himself to one side, felt himself connect with a body there, but the level kept rising.

Christian took a final breath as the water reached his nose, holding it in as he tried desperately to escape the crushing pain in his lungs. As the cool liquid touched his eyelids, he could hold his breath no longer. He choked, spasming in agony as he screamed for air, mouth opening instinctively. Water rushed down his throat, sucked into his lungs. In the moment before he died, Dr Christian Monro felt the fingers of the ghosts clawing at him, echoes of Bedlam with twisted faces, dragging him down to the depths of their Hell.

CHAPTER 1

DETECTIVE SERGEANT JAMIE BROOKE took a deep breath, steeling herself to face the crime scene. It was her first major case since her compassionate leave had come to an end, and although she craved the intellectual stimulation, part of her just wanted to huddle under the covers at her flat and shut out the world. Thoughts of her daughter, gone only three months now, intruded at every second. Jamie welcomed them, but if she let them intensify too much, she knew she would just break down. Not quite the look she favored in front of her work colleagues. Detective Constable Alan Missinghall stood outside the squad car, finishing his morning coffee and sticky bun, waiting for her to join him on the pavement. All Jamie had to do was step out and accompany him to the scene.

Missinghall had been tremendous support during the events a few months ago that culminated in the flames of the Hellfire Caves, and she was grateful for his friendship. Despite her seniority in the force, he was one of the only allies she had after years of insistent independence that protected her from gossip but left her mostly alone. Jamie pulled down the mirror and checked her dark hair, tucking a few strands into the tight bun she habitually wore for work. Her face was gaunt, cheekbones angular, and her pale skin was dull from too long inside during the British winter. *Time to get back out there again*, she thought. Jamie exhaled slowly and opened the door, pulling her coat tightly around her against the chill of the early morning.

"The body was found in one of the offices in the oldest part of the building," Missinghall said, walking slowly, as his six-foot-five frame meant his stride was double Jamie's. "This place has changed substantially since the days of Bedlam. That's for sure."

The Imperial War Museum had been built in the early nineteenth century to house the Bethlem Royal Hospital, known to history as Bedlam. Although the hospital for the mentally ill was relocated in 1930 to the outer suburbs of Kent, this place remained the hospital of the imagination, a virtual horror movie set. Jamie shivered as she glanced up at the cupola rising above a classical facade, but it was the massive First World War guns that drew her attention, dwarfing the uniformed officers already onsite. Each huge naval gun weighed one hundred tons and could fire shells over sixteen miles. Its yellow bullet-shaped ammunition stood around the gardens, each waist height. Jamie couldn't help but touch the spiked top of one of them, a testament to man's ingenuity at designing killing machines. While this place was once a supposed restorer of minds, it was now a home for weapons of mass destruction. A building in homage to war, perhaps the ultimate form of collective madness.

"The museum is currently undergoing massive restoration," Missinghall said. "They're sprucing it up in time for the centennial of the First World War, so the main galleries aren't open to the public right now."

"How was the body found?" Jamie asked.

"One of the workmen was looking for a quiet place to smoke as it was pouring with rain outside." Missinghall chuckled. "He would have needed a few more ciggies after that."

They walked towards the steps leading up to the museum entrance, passing a slab of concrete with a graffitied face and the slogan 'Change Your Life' tattooed on its tongue. Its eyes were manic, the open maw a frozen scream. Jamie bent to read the plaque, and saw it was from the Berlin Wall, a remnant of that divide between East and West Germany. This was a strange place indeed, aimed at commemoration without intentionally glorifying violence.

The sound of a little girl giggling whispered on the wind. Jamie looked up sharply, her eyes drawn to the trees beyond the memorial. Polly ran there, her blue dress caught by the breeze as she twirled amongst the early spring flowers. For a moment, hope filled Jamie's heart, but then the girl's face changed. It was another girl, alive and vibrant, where her daughter was gone. Polly was ashes now, her physical remains in a terracotta urn that sat on the shelf in her flat.

Jamie choked back her emotion and turned to follow Missinghall, who was nearing the main entrance. These moments still threatened to overwhelm her, even months after Polly's death. *Is it self-harm or self-care to want to hurt myself?* Jamie wondered. Pain is a reminder of continued life, and every day she had to make a decision about carrying on.

The craving for a cigarette was intense, her hands shaking a little at the thought. Jamie thrust one hand in her coat pocket, clutching the tin where she put the menthol butt ends, measuring her addiction. She could hardly fit the lid on by the end of the day, but right now she resisted the yearning to smoke, clenching her fist around the tin instead. She wanted to get back to the capable woman she was known as in the force. She just needed to gather her strength.

Jamie and Missinghall went through the main entrance, showing their warrant cards to the officer on the door. The crime-scene perimeter was much further inside the museum, and they walked through a warren of building works, preparation for a grand opening at the centenary of the First World War. It was organized chaos, the kind of place that would be a nightmare to process for evidence, especially with the tight deadlines for the centennial. After winding through corridors, they reached a doorway where they logged into the crime scene and put on the protective coveralls necessary to stop contamination.

The body was still in situ and a number of Scene of Crime Officers (SOCOs) worked efficiently in the room, processing the scene. Jamie tilted her head to one side, her curiosity piqued by the strange tableau. A familiar prick of interest penetrated the haze of grief and she knew that this case was just what she needed to take her mind off her own pain.

The room smelled of candle smoke overlaid with a damp, fungal aroma. A man sat in an oversize wooden chair, his feet bound to the struts and his arms strapped to the sides. His head was entirely covered by a box made of dark wood, so the victim looked more like a dummy from the London Dungeon than a real dead body. He wore a white shirt under a dark tailored suit, and it looked like his clothes were damp. The straps that held his wrists made his suit wrinkle, and his fingertips were bloody, nails cracked, as if he had tried to claw his way out of the chair. Jamie shivered at the thought of being trapped there, unable to move, unable to escape.

Forensic pathologist Mike Skinner stood against the wall, looking at his watch every minute, as if that would hurry the SOCOs. Finally the photos were complete, the device swabbed, and the body could be moved.

Missinghall helped Mike unfasten the straps that held the box in place and together they lifted it off. The victim's head fell forward, unsupported now, onto his chest. A rush of water cascaded down and a SOCO darted forward to capture a sample. Jamie glimpsed ivory padding inside as Missinghall laid the box on the floor for SOCOs to process further. Mike unstrapped the man's arms and legs, fastening forensic bags over the exposed flesh to protect any evidence.

Missinghall helped him to lift the body into a plastic body-bag on top of a waiting gurney. The man looked professorial, authority still held in his bearing even in death. He wasn't a large man, his frame short and compact, not fat but clearly more used to a lecture theatre than a gym. His hair was grey, still wet, and his lips were grey.

"First impressions?" Jamie asked.

"Drowned, I'd say," Mike replied, his curt response purely professional. "But I'll know more after I check his lungs back at the morgue."

Missinghall moved to the gurney and with gloves on, opened the man's jacket. From the top pocket, he pulled out a thick envelope and placed it in a clear plastic evidence bag, a wad of cash visible inside.

"This wasn't theft, that's for sure," Missinghall said, delving back into the man's pockets. He pulled out a thin leather wallet containing a couple of bank cards and a driver's license.

"Doctor Christian Monro," he read. "That makes things easier." He looked over at Jamie, one eyebrow raised. "Guess I'll get on with the preliminary statements then. I'll start with the security team."

A bustling came from the door, and one of the uniformed officers beckoned Jamie over to the edge of the crime-scene markers. A man stood there, shuffling from one foot to another, wringing his hands, eyes darting to the gurney inside the room.

"I'm Michael Hasbrough, the curator of the museum," he blustered. "This is terrible, terrible. You have to keep the press away. The centennial is only in a few weeks, and there's a Fun Run today, as well. It's going to get busy outside soon. You have to hurry up. Please."

Jamie put out a hand to calm the man.

"We need to process the scene properly, Mr Hasbrough. It will take some time, but of course, we'll try to be discreet."

He shook his head violently. "How can you be discreet with a damn body and all those uniforms outside?" Hasbrough seemed to realize what he had said. "With respect to the dead, of course." He glanced into the room again, his eyes taking in the scene more fully. "Perhaps I can help." He pointed towards the box on the floor next to the unusual chair. "I can tell you what that is."

"Go on," Jamie said.

"It's called a Tranquilizer. The device was used on mentally ill patients to calm them down back when this place was the old Bedlam Hospital. They were strapped in and the box placed on their head. The padding stopped any light or sound, like a primitive sensory deprivation tank. Water was sometimes poured over the head of the patient while they were in the box. Apparently it was meant to relax them." He grimaced. "Can't see why though."

"Sounds more like a kind of waterboarding," Jamie said, wondering what the victim might have done to deserve such treatment.

The curator nodded. "There are reports of people dying in the device, of course, but then much of the early treatment for mental illness was inhumane by today's standards. It was designed for control and restraint rather than rehabilitation of any kind."

"Do you have those reports here?" Jamie asked.

Hasbrough shook his head. "No, everything to do with Bedlam is at the hospital. It has moved a number of times over its dark history. Now it's at Beckenham in Kent, a lovely campus, nothing like the cold Gothic place this would have been."

"And this room?" Jamie asked. "Was it part of the old hospital?"

The curator nodded, relaxing as he shared his field of expertise. "Yes, the museum has been substantially altered since it was a hospital but this is one of the old wings. It could have been a treatment room, but we'd have to check the old plans to make certain."

Jamie turned to look back into the room. "So where did the chair come from?"

"We still have some old artifacts in the basement storerooms, and many of them have been cleared out recently for the renovations. This chair could have been easily moved within the museum. It's not a heavy device, as you can see."

Jamie glanced around at the corners of the surrounding corridor.

"Are there any cameras in this part of the building?"

Hasbrough shook his head. "Unfortunately not. We're redoing all the security but because this is under renovation, the cameras were all taken down."

"Someone must have seen this man come in," Jamie said.

The curator nodded. "Perhaps, but we've never had any problems here before. You can't just walk off with a tank or a plane, after all."

Mike Skinner finished the initial processing of the body, covered it and fastened the straps on the gurney. As he rolled it towards the door, the wheels squeaked on the tiled floor. Hasbrough moved back, his nostrils flaring like a skittish horse, as if the mere presence of the body could contaminate him somehow.

"Can you at least take it out the back way?" he asked as the body was rolled past. Skinner ignored the man, heading towards the main entrance. "There are children out there," Hasbrough called. "Bloody half term. Always a crazy time."

"What's going on today?" Jamie asked.

"It's a charity Fun Run for Psyche – you know, that politician Matthew Osborne's thing. Advocates for equality and justice for the mentally ill, or something like that. They got permission for the event months ago. Thought it might be an appropriate place given the history here, and the new hospital is too far out for the press to bother going. But here, there will be some attention and Osborne knows the strings to pull, for sure. I think he's even running today, along with a load of yummy mummies and their brats, no doubt. There are hundreds of people due to turn up, raising money for charity. Be hell to shut it down now."

Jamie glanced down at the plans of the museum she had on her smartphone.

"It looks like the field is far enough away from the crime scene that we don't need to stop it, but we'll need statements from all the people who were here early, including your staff."

Hasbrough nodded. "Of course."

Jamie turned back to the room, watching the SOCOs go about their work, seeing Missinghall on the phone. He waved his hand at her as he began to read the registration details from the driver's license, clearly not needing her right now.

"Can you show me the outside of the building?" she asked Hasbrough.

"Sure, follow me."

Walking out into the fresh air, Jamie breathed in deeply. The sun was peeking through the clouds and it looked like the day might brighten up. Volunteers were hanging bunting around the bushes, putting up Psyche signs and big arrows pointing to the field beyond the museum where the Fun Run would be. A blast of rock music came from the speakers, swiftly muted. Heads turned briefly and then returned to staring at the police vehicles in the forecourt. Jamie had no doubt that gossip about the murder would be round the group in no time.

"There's a back way into the museum," Hasbrough said, walking left from the main building.

"What time would this lot have started setting up?" Jamie asked, counting more than twenty volunteers across the field.

"Some of them were already here when I arrived at six," he said. "That Petra Bennett is some kind of superwoman, I swear it. She was ordering the lads around, getting the stage set up." He pointed across the field towards a figure in shades of moss green and gold, the colors of the charity. Her mousy hair caught a ray of sun, and she brushed an almost-blonde strand from her face, the gesture impatient, as she bent to lift another box.

"The Fun Run starts at ten a.m., so they'll be packing up again by two. Will you have to disturb them?"

Jamie watched Petra speaking to a young volunteer, her hand gestures fast as she pointed down the field. Here was a woman who knew what was going on, and a potential suspect.

"We'll need a list of everyone who was onsite this morning, and then the team will be taking some statements." Jamie saw his disturbed glance. "But we'll try to keep it low key."

They walked on a little way.

"This is the back entrance and the one I use." Hasbrough pointed at a cream safety door. "It was unlocked this morning, but to be honest, it usually is. George, the main night watchman, comes out for a smoke now and then. You can keep time by his addiction."

Jamie clenched her fists as the wave of longing for her own cigarettes swept over her.

"What time does he usually come out here?"

"Every hour on the hour. You can check that with him, but I reckon it gets him through the nights when nothing happens. And nothing ever happens, Detective." Hasbrough paused. "At least, it didn't use to."

As they walked back to the main entrance, Jamie saw a man arrive on the other side of the field, his arms laden with bags and balancing a box in one hand. Petra ran to help him, and a smile lit his face. Jamie had seen Matthew Osborne before on TV, that slightly crooked smile flashed for the press, the gaunt jaw highlighted by an artful line of stubble. He was Secretary of State for Health, but the papers were more interested in his love life. Jamie didn't pay too much attention to politics, but she could see how this man fit right in, as he leaned into Petra and kissed her cheek. She was like a dull little bird, eager to help him, fluttering around his bright plumage. She wondered if he had that effect on all women.

For a moment, Jamie envied Matthew's easy way with people, thinking of her own inability to get close to anyone. It used to be her and Polly against the world, mother and daughter bound together, but now Polly was gone. Fighting the world alone was like standing under a freezing shower all day every day, and sometimes she was beaten to her knees by its force.

Jamie's phone buzzed and she turned from the field to check the text. Today's picture was a clear milk bottle on a red brick step, a daffodil sticking out at a jaunty angle. As usual, Blake had signed it with a smiley. Jamie grinned. For a moment, she felt the darkness in her mind lift a little. Since Polly's death, Blake had kept his physical distance, but every day he let her know he was thinking of her. That alone meant a lot, but she still couldn't see him, for he had a gift. Blake's ability to read emotions in objects meant he would feel the depth of her loss, and she was afraid she would break if he knew.

"Jamie, I've got an address. It's in Harley Street," Missinghall called as he left the museum entrance, walking towards them. "The guy was a psychiatrist. His housekeeper can let us in."

"OK," Jamie said. "Let's go check it out."

CHAPTER 2

BLAKE DANIEL SMILED AS he walked across Great
Russell Street into the courtyard of the British Museum. He
put his phone in his pocket and pulled his thin gloves back
on, covering the scars on his hands. It pleased him to send
Jamie jolly pictures each day and, although she only ever
responded with a smiley in return, he knew that at some
point she would emerge from her grief. He wanted to be
there when she did. Jamie had become a talisman against
his own oblivion, and the nights when he craved the tequila
bottle were becoming ever more rare. She was worth waiting
for.

Blake looked up at the facade of the British Museum, the
tall Ionic columns stretching to the Greek-style pediment,
a fitting entrance to the myriad wonders within. The glass
roof to the Great Court was now fully repaired from the
Neo-Viking attack last month, and the public were streaming in again. The day he stopped loving this place was the
day he ought to retire, Blake thought.

He bounded up the steps into the tourist throng, eyes wide
and clutching maps as they wondered where to start their
day's adventure. Blake loved to try and guess where people
came from. Those who journeyed here to stay in multicul-
tural London had intermingled into one great family that

managed to rub along together most of the time. Sporadic fights broke out, of course, for a family must hate as well as love, as in all the best Shakespeare plays. But that made life more interesting. Blake's own features were mixed, just as his cultural heritage was. He had the tight curly hair of his Nigerian mother, which he kept at a military number-one cut, and blue eyes of the northern ocean from his Swedish father. With his darker skin tone and boy-band features, he could walk with confidence in any part of London.

Swiping his pass by the door, Blake walked downstairs to the offices of the museum, where researchers worked on artifacts for the exhibits above. There was a sense of excitement here, overlaid with the calm of academia, as the minutiae of past civilizations were dissected. Blake was one of a number of researchers, but his work was supplemented by his peculiar sensitivities. It was called clairvoyance by some, or psychometry, although Blake preferred extrasensory perception, and for him, it manifested as a series of visions gleaned from an object. Their intensity was dictated by the emotions that had attached themselves to the artifact over time, so the more personal the item, the more clearly he could read it. He habitually wore thin gloves to cover his skin so as not to be overwhelmed by the visions from daily life, those gloves serving the dual purpose of hiding disfiguring scars from a childhood of abuse.

Walking through the office towards his own workspace, Blake's eyes fixed on the object that lay upon a white cloth on his desk. He had been assigned the fourteenth-century Nubian cross of Timotheus, and he couldn't get a reading on it at all. Perhaps it was a good thing – perhaps he had been relying on the visions too much, before trying to back up his claims with proper research. But his vivid writing certainly brought in the grants, as it captured the imagination of donors with his description of characters who might have been involved in the object's history. They weren't to know how much of it was truth discovered through emotional perception.

Blake sat down in front of the cross, studying the cloverleaf ends, triple hoops of iron in a simple, functional design. Maybe the passage of time had somehow cleansed the cross of its resonance, or perhaps the priests had worn gloves as part of devotional garments. Nubia had been converted to Christianity in the sixth century and had a rich cultural heritage, although the area was now split between Egypt and Sudan, both Muslim countries. This cross could give an insight into an area of Africa that had once been dominated by Christianity, with powerful empires that many would not believe of the fractious continent these days.

"How's your paper going?"

The voice startled Blake and he turned to see Margaret, his boss, standing behind him. She held a small package in a white padded bag.

"I'd like a draft by the end of next week."

Her face was pinched, but that wasn't unusual. Blake knew he skated near the edge with her, and his frequent absences due to hangover recovery had been noted. Tequila and a string of empty one-night stands had made him almost a part-time employee, but in the last few months he had been a lot more reliable. Perhaps Margaret was softening towards him.

"Of course," he said. "I'm still working on researching Timotheus from the Coptic scrolls. I found a new translation yesterday so I'll use that as part of the paper."

Margaret nodded, and held out the package.

"This came for you. But you really shouldn't have personal items delivered to the museum." She frowned. "You know what a nightmare security is with all the random objects we're sent."

Blake took the parcel. "Sorry, I didn't order anything, so I don't know why …"

His voice trailed off as he recognized his mother's sloping handwriting on the front.

"I'll leave you to it then," Margaret said after waiting a beat too long, clearly interested in what was inside.

Blake laid the package down on his desk. Why would his mother post anything? They hadn't spoken in years, and although he sent cards now and then, telling her he was OK, he hadn't mentioned his address or where he worked. Of course, Google meant that everyone was discoverable online these days: his academic papers had been in some journals and his photo was on the museum website. Blake wanted to rip off the paper to find out what was inside, but some part of him held back. Whatever this was, it drew him to a part of his life he had left behind long ago.

One of the meeting rooms was empty, so Blake took the package and walked inside, shutting the blinds and closing the door. He took his gloves off and looked at his hands, the ivory scars on his caramel skin like an abstract painting. Scars his father had inflicted in an attempt to beat the Devil from his son, believing the visions to be diabolical possession and Blake's hands a portal to Hell. But the bloody whippings had only curbed the visions until the scars began to heal, and then they returned, a curse that no amount of pain could stop.

It had been fifteen years since he had walked out on the abuse, turning away from his father and the religious community that he ruled with an iron rod, like the Old Testament prophets he had preached of in his sermons. But his mother … Blake blinked away the tears that threatened as guilt rose inside. He had to leave her, for there had been no other way. His father would rather have killed him than let the Devil take his son, or at least cut off his hands to stop the visions. And, as much as his mother loved him, she had been a devoted wife and servant, believing that it was God's will Blake be delivered from the curse by His prophet. Perhaps there was a trace of her here.

Laying his hands on the parcel, Blake closed his eyes to let the visions come. He was clean, no tequila for days, so his sensitivity was acute. He felt a rising anxiety, like a high-pitched note that hurt his ears, but under that lay a deep acceptance, a sense of peace in a faith he had no connection to. He saw a front door, the same one he had walked out years ago, and a woman's hand, older now, clutching the envelope. He wanted to see her face, wanted more than this brief glimpse into her world. Then he saw a drip, a series of medical machines, and heard a rasping gasp. He knew that voice. Blake pulled his hand away, heart pounding in his chest.

He ripped open the package and looked inside. A white cloth was wrapped around an object and there was a note, just one page. He pulled it out.

My son. There's too much to say and no time left anymore. I'm sorry. Your father has had a series of strokes. Please come. We love you.

Blake read the note again, unsure what he was supposed to feel. He wanted more from her, more than just these few lines after so long. *Why do children read so much into the words of parents?* he thought. *Why expect so much, when they are just people, damaged and desperate, just as we are?* Blake shook his head – the years apart should have given him more perspective.

The old man was dying, that much was certain. Maybe he was dead already, but the thought didn't leave Blake feeling any lighter. On the day he had walked out, Blake had sworn to dance on the old man's grave, wanting to stamp his boots onto the earth as if it had been the prophet's face. But over time, those feelings had hardened into a tight ball of anger that he kept locked up and buried within. The tequila helped soften it, helped him to breathe, but it was a bitch of a mistress that brought as much pain as it did relief.

He needed to know – which meant he had to look more closely. Blake pulled on one of his gloves, not quite ready to experience visions from whatever was in the package. He reached in and took out an object wrapped in a white handkerchief. Blake remembered how his father had always worn one, ironed perfectly into a pocket square for his suits. *A man should dress for his station*, he would say, *the Lord demands us to be our best.* An English affectation, Blake thought with a short smile. Perhaps it said more about his father's immigrant sensibilities than anything the Lord demanded.

The handkerchief was wrapped like a parcel. Blake slowly pulled the edges away to reveal his father's watch, a vintage Patek Philippe, the gold of its face tarnished and the leather strap worn, but still a beautiful piece. Blake's chest tightened and he concentrated on breathing, as a flash of memory took him back. He knelt at the altar while the Elders prayed aloud in tongues, his father's right hand slamming down the cane. Blake's eyes fixed on this watch on his father's left wrist, knowing the time it took to reach the bloody end of his penance and weeping while the seconds ticked away. He felt an echo of pain in his hands and he rubbed them, clenching his fists together as if holding hands with his past self might steel him to the memory.

The watch had been his grandfather's, and his father only took it off at night. For this to leave his wrist for any longer meant that he was seriously ill. Had he asked for it to be sent? Did his father want to see him? Or would it just be a final agony to know that Blake was still an outcast from his family, still considered to be of the Devil. Old age would not lessen the man's fundamental beliefs, but only make them more extreme. The strokes themselves would be seen as an attack from Satan, the tribulations of Job perhaps, and Blake imagined the church praying for their leader, interceding with God for His divine intervention. The reality was that his father was an old man.

Blake exhaled slowly, trying to calm his heart rate. The anxiety that gripped him even at the thought of his father seemed ridiculous now, yet still it held him fast. He wanted to touch the watch and feel something of what his father experienced, but he was also afraid of what he might see. When he was young, he had seen visions from his parents' things – he couldn't help it living in their house. But the glimmers of lust and violence from his father and the shuttered, rigid calm from his mother had frightened him. That's when Blake had first taken to wearing gloves, when his hands weren't bandaged from the beatings.

He took his glove off again and set a five-minute alarm on his smartphone. Sometimes the visions were too much, and he could be lost in overwhelming sights and sounds that left him on the brink of collapse. Sometimes Blake wondered if he should see a psychiatrist about his experiences, but he pushed away the fleeting doubts about his own sanity. These days, his reading helped to solve crimes. He remembered reading the ivory Anatomical Venus figurine with Jamie present and how she had pulled his hand away from the object, helping him out of the trance. But she wasn't here right now, and Blake wanted to see into his father's life. He needed to know whether he should go home and face his childhood fears.

Placing his hands over the watch, Blake gently laid them down, his fingertips connecting with the cool metal on the edges of the face and the smooth glass that covered it. Despite the scars, his sensitivity had only increased with age and experience. Blake let the visions come in a rush, breathing slowly as they swirled about him, glimpses of life flashing by. He sifted through the stream of impressions that assaulted his mind.

He went into the most recent remembrance, the raw emotion of a man crippled by multiple strokes, an awareness of mortality and fear of dying overlaid with too much pride to acknowledge the truth of the end. Blake looked out at the bedroom in his old house, but it was no longer the room he remembered.

The walls sprouted with black growths like nodes of cancer in a smoker's lung, spotted with dull green mold. In places, trickles of liquid ran down, pooling on the bare floorboards in patches of tainted burgundy, like diseased blood. Above the fireplace, one of the lumps moved and Blake realized it was a living creature. The hairs rose on the back of his neck as he perceived a bony spine and tail with skin like tar, the thing's face jagged and its eyes bright with lust for death. It shifted, its gaze lighting on the bed. Blake felt its stare invade his body, examining every cell for a sign of the inevitable end. He heard a moan and knew his father had made the sound: it was all he could utter. But there was no exorcism, no prayers he could invoke to cleanse the room of this filth. Hooded lids closed again as the dark creature waited. Blake sensed that it wouldn't be long now before it would feed.

He tried to see past the creatures and the corruption of the room. Was this some kind of hallucination, a manifestation of his father's worst fears, brought on by the stroke? Or could it be that he was seeing past the physical world into the spiritual realm? If that was true, then the God his father had served for a lifetime had forsaken him, for the room was filled with terror and the promise of Hell.

Blake pulled back, filtering the memories that were attached to the watch. He perceived an overwhelming sense of fear that overlaid everything, a panic barely held back by the violence of his father's fervent prayer and brimstone preaching. It was something he had never expected, for Magnus Olofsson had been the definition of strength, a watchtower the needy had run to for leadership and shelter. That fortitude had been the basis of respect in their community, where perspectives and lifestyles were held over from days long past. When Blake had walked out, he had changed his name as a final separation. Daniel Blake Olofsson had become Blake Daniel, and disappeared to a new life.

In the vision, he saw his mother's face, her eyes closed in prayer, and he felt his father's guilt as he looked at her. The emotion was so strong that Blake pulled away from the sensation quickly. He couldn't stand to know what his father was guilty of, not right now. But he held back from leaving the trance completely.

He had to go there, he realized. He had to return to the place he had run from years ago, and so Blake parted the veils of memory. He saw his own face as a young boy, kneeling by the altar in the church, tears running down as men surrounded him. He felt the righteous rage inside his father, but that anger wasn't directed at Blake, his son, it was at the Devil for taking him. Blake felt an echo of his father's thoughts as blood dripped onto the altar, *He punishes the children and their children for the sin of the parents to the third and fourth generation.*

The alarm pierced Blake's thoughts and he anchored his mind on it, pulling his hands away as he returned to the room under the British Museum again. Why was the verse from the book of Numbers in his father's mind as he labored with the cane? What sin had his father committed that God would punish his child for atonement?

CHAPTER 3

HARLEY STREET HAD LONG been noted for its private medical practices, and the very name resonated with old money and privilege. Number 37 was on the corner of Queen Anne Street, a Victorian five-story house with ornate windows. Jamie glanced up to the sculptures on the facade, displaying a laurel-crowned figure with volumes of Homer and Milton, and a reclining young man with a telescope and a star. Poetry and astronomy seemed curiously out of place on this street of medical history.

Missinghall unfolded himself from the police car, beginning his second morning pastry and offering Jamie a bite. His large frame meant he was always eating, and he chipped away at trying to get Jamie to eat more, tempting her with little morsels. Her clothes were loose around her hips now, and she often forgot to eat until she was nauseous with hunger by the end of the day. The physical reminder of her body's insistence for life was something she danced on the edge of resisting. Jamie had read that the Jain religion had a ritual death by fasting, and the vow of *sallekhana* could be taken when an individual felt their life had served enough of a purpose: when there were no ambitions or wishes left and no responsibilities remained. Some days, Jamie wanted to embrace such an end, but Polly had told her to live, to dance, and her responsibility was still to bring justice to the dead. But was that enough of a purpose to keep her going?

It would have to be for today, Jamie thought, and accepted the offer of pastry with a smile. Missinghall broke off a generous piece and Jamie forced it down her throat, the act of swallowing almost against her will.

"There should be a housekeeper here," Missinghall said, brushing crumbs from his suit. Jamie noticed that he had red socks on today, peeking out from under his slightly too-short trousers, his way of bringing color to their dark work. "She manages the place for the practitioners."

Jamie pressed the buzzer and after a moment, the door opened. A slim woman in jeans and a Rolling Stones t-shirt stood at the entrance, her cropped ash-blonde hair belying her middle age. Jamie showed her warrant card and introduced herself and Missinghall.

"Of course, I was expecting you," the woman said. "What a business. Dr Monro dead. Well, I never." She shook her head. "Come in, come in. I haven't touched anything in his rooms, just like the officer told me on the phone."

She led them into the hallway.

"How many practices are there here?" Jamie asked.

"Four," the housekeeper said. "They keep themselves to themselves, and I look after all their rooms. Not that any of them are much trouble, you know."

"Any tension between the businesses at all?"

The woman turned on the first step of the stairs.

"Not that I would know about, Detective. But then I'm just the housekeeper now, aren't I?"

Despite her words, Jamie could see a cloud in her blue eyes. There was more here, but perhaps the rooms themselves would help set the scene before she pushed any harder.

On the second floor, the housekeeper unlocked a wooden door, inset with two half panes of stained glass featuring red and blue art deco roses.

"You can look around, and please take all the time you need, Detectives. I'll come back in a bit. Would you like tea?"

"Yes, please," Missinghall jumped at the chance. "We're both black, one sugar."

Jamie stepped into the room, pulling on a pair of sterile gloves as Missinghall did the same behind her.

She had expected a cozy nook with a couch and blankets, somewhere welcoming for private therapy. Instead, the rooms were fashioned in a Japanese minimalist style, with just two chairs and a small table in one main space and a study beyond. The walls were a light cream, with nothing to decorate the space. It was entirely blank, offering the patient no respite from their own mind.

Walking into the study area beyond, Jamie noted the filing cabinets of patient records and a general neatness and organization. There were thick medical textbooks on a bookshelf as well as a framed degree certificate, and a couple of files and a fountain pen lay on a desk of Brazilian walnut. In the corner was a small fridge, topped with a kettle and coffee plunger. On the wall, a single large canvas showed a blue ocean with white-capped waves. On first glance, the waters seemed calm, but as Jamie looked at it more closely, she noticed the darkening skies towards the edge of the painting as a storm approached. Under the waves there were shadows, darker patches of blue that could have been creatures of the depths. It was a strange painting, perhaps one of Monro's analysis tools, the shadows interpreted according to the viewer's perspective. Jamie imagined sharks there, with razor teeth to shred her flesh, but she still felt an urge to sink under the blue.

Missinghall walked to the back of the study, where another door led onwards. He turned the handle. It was locked.

"That's his private apartment," the housekeeper said, walking in with the tea and a plate of biscuits. "I was never allowed in there. He was particular about that."

"Did he live as well as work here, then?" Jamie asked.

"Let's just say he didn't have a routine that meant he left his rooms too much." She hesitated. "I think that was a problem with some of the other partners in the building. He needed heating, electricity and other amenities at night, and never paid more than his allotted percentage. But of course, the other practices have wonderful people in them. None of them could possibly be involved in his murder."

Jamie smiled, helping her with the tea things. "Of course."

"I'll come back in a bit then, see if you need anything else."

"Thank you."

As she left, Missinghall pulled an evidence bag from his pocket, a bunch of keys visible inside.

"I thought we might be needing these," he said. "They were in Monro's jacket pocket."

Using the bag as a second glove, he maneuvered the keys, trying them against the lock for size until one fitted. He turned the key and pushed open the door.

"Ladies first," he smiled at Jamie, and she nodded her head, walking through ahead of him. It was dark inside, the windows shaded, so it was hard to see at first. As Missinghall flicked on the light, Jamie gasped at what they saw.

The room was dominated by a gynecological bed in the center, with green padded cushions and the addition of leather straps at each end, as well as stirrups and supports. Under the table was a wooden box. Missinghall lifted the lid to reveal a number of different crops, whips, eye masks and a ball gag.

"Bloody hell, I wasn't expecting that," Missinghall said, eyebrows raised. "I thought this guy was a psychiatrist, not some kind of sexual services provider."

"He was only supposed to be interested in their minds," Jamie said, walking around the bed. "But clearly, he liked to take things a little further."

She walked to a desk near the shaded window and turned on the lamp. A large leather notebook lay in pride of place, with a serpent-green fountain pen beside it. Jamie opened the book, examining Monro's handwriting within. The last page was an account of a session with a client he called 'M,' noting her response to the discipline and how many strokes she had endured. There were some musings about the efficacy of physical restraint on the mad, how they were more comfortable being punished than being left alone to get well, and how perhaps the original Bedlam had been correct in chaining the inmates. There were quotes from a Dr George Henry Savage: *I would rather tie a patient down constantly than keep him always under the influence of a powerful drug … The scourging of the lunatic in times past might have occasionally been a help to recovery.*

Jamie frowned as she flicked through the pages, seeing multiple entries over the last month, the same initials appearing several times. Were these willing participants in Monro's extra services, or did he use his position of power to coerce his clients? Was one of them responsible for his death?

Above the desk was a bookshelf with four more of the large journals. Jamie pulled another one down, finding the same type of information but with other initials. Monro had clearly been doing this for years, so it was conceivable that patients had come to him specifically for this kind of treatment. Complaints about his professionalism would have shut him down a long time ago otherwise.

"You'll want to see this, Jamie."

She turned to see Missinghall looking into a large walk-in closet. He moved aside to let her enter. A wall-size cabinet dominated the space, filled with all kinds of pharmaceuticals, some regulated substances, others common antidepressants and antipsychotics. None of them should have been kept on the premises in such large doses.

"He was dealing, as well? What wasn't this guy into?" Missinghall shook his head, moving over to check one of the filing cabinets, his gloved fingers flicking through the tabbed index.

Jamie sighed. "We're going to have to go through his list of clients, past and present. Clearly the murder was related to madness somehow, but it could have also been about sex or drugs."

"I don't think it was money, though," Missinghall said, holding up a bank statement. "His balance is unhealthier than mine."

Jamie frowned. "Which doesn't fit with the implication of selling drugs directly. So where's the money?"

There was a ring on the doorbell, and they heard the steps of the housekeeper and then her voice, faint from downstairs. The tread of two sets of footsteps ascended to the second floor. Jamie went back into the main room, pulling the door of the inner sanctum closed, leaving Missinghall to continue to go through paperwork. The housekeeper knocked and then pushed open the door to the practice rooms.

"Detective, there's a Mr Harkan here. He says it's impor-tant."

Harkan was thin and fair, with the rosy cheeks of a choirboy who had never quite grown up. He put out a grace-ful hand to introduce himself to Jamie as the housekeeper headed off downstairs again.

"I'm sorry, Detective, but this couldn't wait. I just heard about the murder – the news is already out, I'm afraid, and Harley Street is a tight-knit community. I'm a solicitor. Our firm is just down the street, and we worked with Monro. He was a forensic psychiatrist as well as a clinical practitioner."

"A man of many talents," Jamie said, thinking of the room out back.

"Indeed," said Harkan, and Jamie noticed his eyes flick

towards the door. Did the solicitor know what lay beyond?

"What exactly did he work with you on?" she asked.

"Forensic psychiatry is the intersection of law and the psychiatric profession, and Monro helped assess competency to stand trial. He was an expert witness around aspects of mental illness, both for the prosecution and the defense. He also assessed the risk of repeat offending."

"So why the hurry to talk to us?" Jamie asked. "You could have come down to the station with a statement."

"It's the timing," Harkan said, wringing his hands. "Monro was an expert witness for the prosecution in the case of Timothy MacArnold a few years back. A violent, repeat offender who claimed mental illness drove his actions, and Monro supported that in his testimony. MacArnold is in Broadmoor, the maximum-security mental health hospital for violent offenders."

"And why are you so worried?"

"MacArnold's case is coming up for review and Monro was trying to get him transferred to some exclusive research hospital. I don't know the exact details of that, but I do know that MacArnold has a good position at Broadmoor and if he wanted to stay there … well, he's a violent man used to getting what he wants, even inside." Harkan's eyes flicked all over the room, beads of sweat forming on his brow. His speech was hurried, tripping over his words in the haste to get them out. Jamie noted his concerns on her pad, but they would have to look at Mr Harkan more closely.

"Then of course there's the families of MacArnold's victims," Harkan continued. "They're livid at the thought of him getting even better treatment than he does now, all art therapy and counseling when he butchered their loved ones. There's a lot of anger at Monro for his support of the insanity plea."

Jamie nodded.

"We're certainly going to investigate all these angles, Mr

Harkan. This is useful information, so I'd like you to give an official statement. My colleague, DC Missinghall will take you through the process and get some more details. If you'd just wait here a minute."

Jamie walked to the back room and ducked inside, careful to shield the inside space from view and closing the door briefly behind her. There was already enough gossip on this street.

"Al, can you take a proper statement from this guy? Apparently Monro was involved in the justice system, as well." She lowered her voice. "And I think we need to investigate his background, too. Seems a little too quick in assigning motive for the murder. Of course, he might just be the neighborhood busybody."

Missinghall groaned. "There's always one. Righto, but seriously, how many motives can there be for murdering this guy?" He handed a thick box file to Jamie. "You'll want to have a look through this. It's his clients, past and present."

Missinghall went out to take Harkan's statement as Jamie perched on the bed, thumbing through the cards in the box. Judging by the dates of the first appointments, they covered the last five years. There were a lot of patients, both male and female, and there were symbols on each card, perhaps a visual reference system enabling Monro to easily follow the development of treatment. But what did those symbols mean?

There were red squares, yellow triangles and a blue shape, like a raindrop, interspersed between the cards. Some had just one and others had multiple symbols. Jamie noticed that a black circle in the upper right coincided with the end of the appointments for an individual. There were also larger pieces of paper folded in between some of the cards. Jamie pulled one out to find an extensive family tree drawn in dark pen, each person labeled with a name and their mental health status. This particular patient had black circles dotted all over the page and Monro had commented in spidery handwriting on the need for intervention to stop the continuation of this family stain.

As she continued to flick through the pack of records, Jamie noticed a name she vaguely recognized. Melyssa Osborne. The card had the red square, blue raindrop and the black circle on it. Why did that name ring a bell?

Jamie got out her smartphone, removed a glove, and searched for the name. Melyssa was the younger sister of MP Matthew Osborne; she had been diagnosed with bipolar disorder and had committed suicide three months earlier. The black circle must mean deceased. Jamie flicked through the pack again and noted how many black circles there were, many of which also had the blue raindrop. Her own work was a dark business, but there was a cemetery's worth in these records. They would need to check on all the patients Monro had treated. Jamie opened Monro's diary and compared the initials to the patients in the last week. Another name leapt out at her. Petra Bennett had attended appointments every week – the same woman who had been at the Imperial War Museum for the Psyche Fun Run and who had greeted Matthew Osborne so warmly.

CHAPTER 4

BACK AT NEW SCOTLAND Yard, Jamie typed her notes up on Monro's office as she considered the new suspects they had added to the list. There was still a long list of people who had been at the Imperial War Museum to interview, and a host of other possible leads. Around it all, the miasma of madness seeped through the evidence, like the freezing fog of a London winter.

Missinghall walked up behind Jamie and placed a small square of chocolate brownie on her desk.

"It's Rory's birthday, and he insisted you eat that."

Jamie felt a wave of nausea to look at it, but she knew Missinghall meant well. Food was a constant in their working relationship, at least. She popped it in her mouth and chewed, forcing the sweetness down, willing the sugar to lift her mood. Missinghall smiled and in his brief moment of pleasure for her, Jamie felt better. At least she was beginning to make some friends in the force now, after years of being distant from her colleagues. At first, her independence had been a way to protect the little time she had left with Polly, and a way to stop herself being hurt again. Her ex-husband, Matt, had ripped her heart out when he had left her to cope with a disabled daughter alone. As the years went by, Jamie had turned her independence into a kind of armor, and doing her job well became more important than friendship. Perhaps that was changing now, since her fellow officers knew about her role in the Hellfire Caves. They also knew that somehow the glory had gone to the senior officer on the case, Detective Superintendent Dale Cameron, and there were rumors he had been offered a more senior role in the last few weeks. Jamie hoped he would move on because his presence still made her uneasy, the way his eyes followed her when she walked past his office.

Jamie still had flashbacks to that night of blood and smoke, when in a drugged haze, she had thought Cameron's face was amongst those who performed the atrocity. He had been protective of her in the aftermath of the investigation, encouraging her return to the force and then making sure she was supervised by his hand-picked team. Jamie had wondered what he was protecting her from, or whether he was merely making sure she wasn't able to report her suspicions. If Cameron moved on, Jamie might be able to breathe again as things returned to something resembling normal. Or at least what was considered normal in the homicide team.

Missinghall flipped open his pad.

"Just heard from Skinner. Time of death was likely between midnight and five a.m. Cause of death was drowning, but the Doc also found a needle stick in the victim's neck and suspects a powerful hallucinogenic drug was used. It will take a while for toxicology to come back though."

Jamie shook her head as she imagined being stuck in that box, strapped down while seeing terrifying visions. It brought back hazy memories of being manacled in the swirling smoke of the Hellfire Caves, unsure of what was real. "So it was torture as well as murder," she whispered.

Missinghall continued. "We've also got the full list of statements from the people who were setting up the Psyche Fun Run that morning. Unsurprisingly, no one saw anything. They were all down the other end of the field because the curator didn't want kids near the flower beds so close to the reopening of the museum." Missinghall shuffled his papers, pulling out a sheaf of statements. "But Monro's financials are interesting. We got hold of his other bank account, the one he was clearly keeping separate. It shows significant payments of large amounts at sporadic intervals. The company they're from traces back to a shell organization that we can't penetrate. There's also substantial transfers for smaller amounts of money at more regular intervals. Interestingly, one of the regular transfers is to Mr Harkan, the solicitor who seemed very keen to point the finger at anyone but himself."

"Right, get him down here," Jamie said. "You can go over that new evidence with him, although killing Monro would seem to make it less likely he would get his ongoing payments."

Missinghall nodded. "I'll also get on with arranging access to Broadmoor so you can check out Timothy MacArnold, although clearly he didn't kill Monro himself. That place is a fortress."

Jamie's phone rang, interrupting their discussion. As she picked up, Detective Superintendent Dale Cameron's smooth voice spoke before she could.

"Can you come through to Interview Room 12, please?"

"Of course, sir. I'll be right through."

Her mind was buzzing as she put down the phone, and she caught Missinghall's quizzical look.

"Something up?" he asked.

"Not sure, but Cameron wants to see me – in an interview room, not his office."

"Duh duh duh, duh-duh duh," Missinghall started in with the Darth Vader theme.

Jamie pushed her chair back, standing up. "Oh, stop it. I'm sure it's nothing."

But she wondered about that night in the Hellfire Caves and what she had really seen. How much of a stake did Cameron have in her career now?

She knocked on the interview room door and went in. Dale Cameron stood as she entered.

"Morning, sir."

"Jamie," Cameron nodded, his patrician silver hair catching the harsh light. He was a striking man for his age, with the looks of a wealthy CEO or career politician. His rise through the ranks of the police was legendary, as was his reputation for Teflon shoulders when it came to avoiding responsibility for disaster.

Jamie glanced at the mirror on the wall, wondering if there was someone behind it. Why else would they be in an interview room with the ability to see in, but with no way to tell who was watching?

"This new case is sensitive," Cameron said. "Especially with the timings around the centennial at the Imperial War Museum."

Jamie nodded. "We're trying to minimize the impact on the museum, sir."

"Of course, of course … but there's something you need to know about Monro, and you need to keep this to yourself." Cameron's eyes were like flecks of diamond and Jamie looked away first, unable to meet his stare. She nodded again and he continued. "Monro was affiliated with a government program investigating ways to reduce the burden of mental health in this country." Jamie almost flinched at his use of the word burden.

"They're also interested in ways to enhance brain function in normal people," Cameron continued.

"And by normal, you mean people who haven't been diagnosed as mentally ill?" Jamie couldn't help herself.

"However you want to define it," Cameron snapped. "Regardless, I need you to communicate any evidence about

Monro's research to me directly. I will be passing it on to the appropriate people concerned."

Jamie looked pointedly at the mirrored panel on the wall.

Cameron's tone softened. "Now Jamie, I know you've had difficulties coming back to work after the death of your daughter. I hope you realize I've been making allowances for your fragile mental state." Jamie wanted to interrupt him, wanted to challenge him, but she knew there was a hint of truth in his words. "Many senior officers said you should have been suspended based on your uncontrolled actions in the Jenna Neville case, but I want to continue to help you … Do you understand?"

Jamie hesitated, meeting his eyes and seeing the blue skies of soaring ambition there. She didn't want to fly that high, especially if it meant compromising her integrity. Eventually, she nodded.

"Of course, sir. I'll report anything I find on Monro's research to you." She stood to leave, the scrape of her chair just a little louder than was necessary. "Will that be all?"

"One more thing," Cameron said. "I've heard you have a … friend … with skills that could be misconstrued by the press should his actions become known."

Jamie felt her cheeks color. She wasn't ashamed of Blake, but she knew how his psychic ability could be interpreted as unprofessional. She had kept his involvement quiet after the Hellfire Caves, but he had visited her in hospital, and he would have been easy enough for Cameron to investigate.

"Yes, sir. But we're just friends, and he has nothing to do with the museum murder."

"Actually, I'm interested in how we could use his skills on this case, Jamie. I don't want to rule anything out and it sounds like you had some good results from his tips before. Can you get him to have a look at the crime scene?"

Jamie was stunned, and not in a good way. Cameron's interest was never for anyone else's benefit.

"Perhaps he will be able to shed some light on the Monro murder?" Cameron continued, and it seemed he was studiously avoiding the mirrored panel on the wall.

"I don't think ..." Jamie protested.

"As I said," Cameron interrupted, his fist clenching on the table between them. "I want to continue to protect your position on the force, and I'd like to hear what your friend has to say."

In moments like these, Jamie wanted to get on her motorbike and just roar away, leave all this political crap behind. But she loved the job, and she had nothing else to live for but bringing justice to the dead. Perhaps Blake would help with the Monro case, but she had to figure out what Cameron wanted with him. She nodded slowly.

"I'll get him down to the crime scene before processing is complete."

"Today, Jamie." Cameron's tone was firm.

She nodded again and walked out of the room, feeling his eyes on her back, her skin bristling with awareness of someone else watching from behind the mirrored panel. Instead of returning to her desk, Jamie ducked into one of the other interview rooms opposite and waited. She was so sure someone else had been watching, and she needed to see who it was. She pushed the door almost closed so she could see out but remain unseen herself.

After a couple of minutes, the interview room door opened and Cameron came out. He pulled open the door to the side room, and said something to the shadows. Another man strode out, taller than Cameron, which made him over six foot two. His head was completely shaved, with a skull that seemed misshapen in some way, a slight asymmetry that made Jamie want to stare for longer. His eyes flicked across to the room opposite and Jamie ducked backwards to avoid his glance, but not before she had seen that he had heterochromia, one eye blue and the other brown. What was this man's involvement with the case, and why did he want Blake to read at the murder scene?

CHAPTER 5

IN THE CAR PARK of the station, Jamie pulled on her protective gear while she considered what she would say to Blake. Her stomach fluttered and she laughed softly to herself at the faint excitement of being with him again. It had been a long time since she had looked forward to seeing a man so much. Jamie took a deep breath and dialed. Blake picked up on the first ring.

"Jamie, are you OK?"

The concern in his tone made her smile.

"I'm fine, and this is actually a work call. I wondered if you might be able to help with another case?" The silence was just a beat too long. "Blake, are you there?"

"Yes, sorry. Of course, I'm just a little distracted today. An object came in and I'm having problems with it."

"Oh, of course, if you're busy …"

"Actually, I could use a change of scene and I'd love to see you. Where shall we meet?"

"The Imperial War Museum on Lambeth Road. Just wait outside and I'll take you in."

"OK. See you there in an hour."

The line went dead as he hung up, and Jamie felt a wave of relief wash over her. Blake's abilities were disturbing, but they also meant that she didn't have to hide with him. He had read her once through a comb that Polly had made for her hair. Blake had seen her daughter's sickness and Jamie's own grief sublimated through tango, a side of her that few had witnessed. He had laid her open and part of her craved his vision into her life. She knew he numbed his own nightmares with tequila, oblivion drowning his darkness, so they were both wounded, both struggling to survive. Perhaps they could at least fight the world together today.

Jamie sat astride her bike and pulled her helmet on. The jet-black BMW was her freedom, not meant to be used on police business. But while the long leash Dale Cameron had given her seemed to still be in effect, Jamie was determined to make the most of it. She revved the bike and pulled out into the London streets.

***

The Imperial War Museum was deliberately imposing, and as Jamie pulled up, she saw Blake standing in front of it, looking up at the great facade. His face was troubled. For a moment, Jamie realized that he had been such a support for her in the last few months, but she hadn't asked him what was going on in his own life. He clearly had his own troubles, but right now she barely had enough strength for her own.

Jamie dismounted, pulling off her helmet and putting it in the panniers along with her leather jacket. Blake stood watching her as she tidied her hair, pulling stray black strands into her fixed style.

"Hey," he said, with a shy half smile, his blue eyes striking against his dark skin.

"Hey yourself," Jamie smiled and leaned in to kiss his cheek, avoiding the intensity of his gaze. She touched his gloved hands, briefly caressing the thin material, stunned by her reaction to seeing him after so long. Part of her wanted to break down in his arms and tune out the world, for there was so much unspoken between them. But now wasn't the time.

"Thanks for coming," she said.

"To be honest, I could really use the distraction."

"Really? Anything I should know about?"

Blake sighed, shaking his head. "I'm not even sure what I'm doing about it myself yet, but I'll let you know. So what do you need from me?"

"I don't want to tell you too much, but this is a crime scene and there was a murder here, so be prepared for that. Dr Christian Monro was a psychiatrist and this place was once known as Bedlam."

Blake looked up at the giant cannons outside the museum. "It still seems to be a house of the mad."

They walked into the museum, Jamie showing her warrant card to the officer on duty. The SOCOs had finished processing the scene earlier, but the place was still secure as the investigation continued. Jamie and Blake eased past the crime-scene tape that was in place within the inner rooms. The quiet was almost tangible after the bustle of the crime scene Jamie had seen early this morning. The smell of the processing materials lingered, underneath it a note of desperation. Or was that just her imagination?

"They're refurbishing the place, so these rooms weren't being used," Jamie said. "The body was discovered by a workman."

As they entered, Blake caught sight of the sturdy chair with leather straps.

"You want me to read that? Seriously, Jamie. It looks like something from a horror movie."

Jamie stood looking at it. "It's called a Tranquilizer, believe it or not. I understand if you don't want to read. I don't think it will be pleasant."

Blake's eyes narrowed as he looked at the device, assessing

the challenge. "I'm not sure that it could be any worse than the Hunterian Museum and all those medical specimens." He peeled the glove off his right hand. "Just keep an eye on me, will you? Pull my hand away if I'm under too long." He placed his bare hand on the wooden arm of the chair and closed his eyes.

Jamie watched him, fascinated with his gift, although she still didn't quite know what to make of it. She had seen evidence that his visions were true in some sense, and they led to information that could be verified independently. His breathing slowed and there was a moment when Blake became absent, as if his life energy disappeared and there was only a body left, not a mind within. He was totally still except for a slight twitching behind his eyelids that made his long eyelashes tremble. It was hard not to study his features as he stood like a statue, a handsome god who suffered the trials of men. Jamie wondered what he was seeing.

***

There was no easing into the veils of memory this time, and Blake reeled as the noise hit him. Like an oncoming train, it started in the distance but rumbled fast into his consciousness, rising to a screech. It was the deafening clamor of people calling for help, moaning their distress, rocking back and forth with self-comforting noises. There was a rattling of chains, and a single voice, deep and resonant, singing a hymn to God, as if the Almighty could step down and open the doors of this prison like he had for St Paul.

The walls around him were damp and, in places, dripping with condensation that made the air muggy and thick. The smell of rotting flesh, of disease and shit and sweat filled the air. Blake became aware of people around him in the room. A skeletal figure, perhaps a woman, was fastened to the wall by a chain attached to a riveted belt around her waist. Her clothes were stained with blood and pus from sores as the restraint rubbed on her skin, and she held a piece of old blanket around her shoulders for warmth. She knelt in the corner, her long, dirty fingernails scratching at the plaster, making little marks. Was she trying to find a way out, or was it just the human need to record the passing of time, the transience of human existence? Another woman sat weeping in the opposite corner, her shoulders shaking with silent grief, and around her, other people rocked back and forward, their moans stifled by fear. The cell was cramped, with no separation between the patients according to their affliction. It was merely containment, preventing these rejects from impinging on polite society.

A long howl came from outside the cell, a sound from the depths of despair when words have ceased to hold meaning. The cacophony was part of the assault of this place of madness. Only the civilized are silent, or appropriate in the sounds they make, but when you were shut in here, Blake thought, how could you not cry out?

The howl came again and then the voice broke down in a scream as the noise of thudding against flesh drowned it out. Blake concentrated on the sound and found himself outside the cell in a corridor, watching as two guards beat a man with short coshes. The man was huddled, arms protecting his head, but the guards continued the beating until they grunted with exertion.

"That'll learn you, fuckin' loon," one of the men said, giving the man a final kick. "Monro don't like all that noise, especially when the ladies are getting their … exercise."

The men laughed, an undercurrent of twisted lust echoing down the halls. Blake started at Monro's name. How could the murdered man be here? These men were dressed in eighteenth-century clothing, and Bedlam Hospital had been moved from this site generations ago. The guards hauled the man back into a cell, his blood leaving a stain on the ground, and Blake followed them down the corridor towards the other half of the building.

Part of Blake's mind saw the museum as it now was, pristine cream walls with elegant paintings and no sense of the past. But the walls of this place were steeped in the suffering of the mad, the mental anguish of those chained up and force fed until their teeth broke. People would come to look at them, laughing through the windows of the cells at the craziness within. There were no witnesses here, no one to hear their screams, no one who could act to save them. So the inmates would plug their ears, singing loudly to block out the sound of collective anguish. Some believed they were in Hell, where their punishment was eternal, and now the echo of those times leached from the walls, a manifestation of the past. The air was thick with expectation, and Blake felt a psychic danger here, a darkness that longed for another soul to add to the tortured throng.

The passageways of the hospital were dark, cornered with shadow. Blake heard sounds of desperation and pain coming from the cells, but as the guards ran their clubs along the walls, the noises quieted. They came to a brighter area with two tiled rooms and Blake felt waves of agony coming from the place. He leaned on the wall as the sensations assaulted him, and then looked inside for the source.

On one side was a kind of operating theatre, but with none of the sterile trappings of modern hospitals. There was a bed with leather straps and a head brace. A tray full of medical instruments lay next to it, with a length of tubing attached to a pump.

On the other side, Blake saw a room for torture sanctioned by science. A man was strapped tightly on a board about to be lowered headfirst into a water bath by two guards. A doctor stood near his head.

"No, please no more." The man moaned, thrashing his

head, panic giving him strength. But the two guards were stronger and held him tight, slowly tilting the board as excitement glinted in their eyes.

"Sshh, sshh," the doctor said, his gestures an attempt at calm. "This treatment will shock your system and restart your consciousness. We'll bring you back and you may be well again. This treatment, *usque ad deliquum*, to the brink of death, has been proven to work in many patients at other hospitals. You're so lucky we've chosen you to try it on."

The doctor nodded his head and the guards tipped the patient so his head and shoulders were fully immersed underwater. Blake counted the seconds, watching as the man thrashed around, feeling the waves of panic and pain emanate from him. The man finally stilled, his limbs going limp, but still the doctor counted on.

"Just a little longer," Blake heard the man say. "We need to make sure the shock is complete."

Blake sensed the victim's spirit lift from his body, exuding relief that this life was over, that he could finally escape. The guards tipped the board up, turned it on its side and released the man's body. The doctor thumped hard on the man's back and the patient vomited up a quantity of water that ran into the central drain. Blake felt the pull of his spirit back to physical life, the resistant despair, and then the patient was coughing and retching, gasping for breath.

The doctor nodded, writing on his chart.

"Excellent, we'll just repeat that to be sure."

The man on the floor was weak but he tried to rise at the words, attempting to drag himself towards the door as his face twisted in desperation at his fate.

"Oh no, you don't," one of the guards said, bringing his boot down heavily on the man's back, pinning him to the floor. "Back on the board with you, crazy bastard. The Doc's just trying to help."

The guard's voice echoed with the enjoyment of a man

who loved to inflict pain and control, and Blake knew that this patient would only find release if they let him drown.

He tried to shift the veils of awareness back to the present time, back to the murder last night. The emotions were so weak in comparison to the people who had been trapped and tortured here long ago, who had died here. But there was a hint in the air, a need for revenge and retribution, for leveling the score on behalf of all those who were lost within these walls. There was also a clarity of thought, a strength of purpose. The mad had been beaten down and abused, judged and tortured for too long and now they had a champion, but Blake couldn't see anything of the details of that particular night.

***

He jolted out of the trance to find Jamie shaking his arm.

"Blake, it's OK. Come back now. Please."

He was lying on the floor, a cold sweat covering his body. He shivered as he centered on the present again. Blake opened his eyes to see Jamie's face close to his. For a moment, he forgot the horror of Bedlam and wanted to tilt his head and kiss her, revel in the moment and leave the past behind. But he knew it was too soon, and he couldn't bear it if she pulled away.

"Water," he whispered, sitting up with her help, leaning against the wall and pulling his gloves back on. His hands were shaking a little, the aftermath of the visions that always rocked him.

Blake drank deeply from the bottle Jamie handed him. He could smell the new paint on the walls and it seemed incongruous after what he had just witnessed. It was just one of the strange sensations of his visions, the present always so different from the past.

Jamie sat next to him on the floor, waiting for him to recover. He could feel her wanting to ask what he had seen, but she held back. After years of hiding his gift, and witnessing people's generally spooked reactions to what he saw, Blake relished Jamie's acceptance of who he really was.

"It seems your Monro was just one in a long line of mind doctors," Blake said. "Although what we would call doctors now seems hardly appropriate for what they were in those days." He pulled his smartphone from his pocket and searched for more on the Monros and Bedlam. "Here, look, the family was in charge of Bedlam for three generations, making their money from madness and hiding those considered inappropriate from society. The final Monro had to resign because he was 'wanting in humanity,' but the entire family was notorious. They prescribed treatments without even seeing patients, and back then, treatments including bleeding, purging and various chemical concoctions to sedate or shock the patient back to health." Blake scrolled down. "See here, the Georgian mad were treated as chained beasts and Monro was responsible for bloodletting, forced vomiting and blistering. Under their administration, Bedlam used chains and restraints, beating and brutality to manage the inmates. There was filthy accommodation, infected sores from chaining, gagging or bandaging of the head to stop talking, force-feeding to such brutality that teeth were missing, jaws broken and reports of rape."

Blake shook his head. "I saw some of this happening, Jamie, and the reports make it seem somehow acceptable because the medical profession allowed it. But what was reported must have been just the tiniest part of the whole."

"I think the abuse still goes on," Jamie said. "I saw evidence of it in Monro's office. The records of one girl indicated suicide after treatment that can't possibly have been sanctioned officially. But what about Monro's murder? Could you see anything about that specifically?"

Blake trailed his gloved fingertips on the patterned tiles on the floor. He shook his head.

"There wasn't much, as the dominant emotions here are the suffering of those thousands before him. But Monro's murder was certainly one of revenge, and there was no sense that the person who did it suffered from any kind of mental illness. It was as if they were clinically detached, coldly aware of what this man's ancestors had done. I don't think you're looking for one of Monro's patients."

Jamie frowned. "But surely to kill him for the sins of past generations seems like the act of someone not entirely rational?"

"Oh, I think this Monro was abusing the so-called mad as much as his ancestors had been. The murder was committed here to honor the dead, a repayment of a debt owed to those society put here to forget." Blake paused for a moment. "There was something else, almost a reckless feeling. I don't think the murderer has anything left to lose."

"You mean they're not finished?"

"If he or she, and I can't tell which, is some kind of Robin Hood for the mad, then yes, I think there will be more incidents."

"And I have no way of finding out who might be next," Jamie said quietly.

Blake took her hand and squeezed it gently.

"You can't fight death, Jamie. You can't take on every criminal in London and expect to stop the violence. Just like I can't fight the past, I can only perceive its passing …"

A buzz interrupted Blake's words. Jamie checked her phone and saw a text from Missinghall.

You're good to go to Broadmoor. All cleared. Have emailed details.

Jamie stood. "Are you heading back to the British Museum now?"

Blake thought of his father's watch, and a shadow crossed

his face. "I might be going away for a few days, actually."

Jamie raised an eyebrow. "Anything you need help with?"

Blake shook his head. "I'm not quite ready to talk about it yet, but I'll text you later."

***

Blake watched as Jamie got on her bike and waved, before revving off into traffic. It made him smile to watch her drive away, all black leather and tough exterior but with so much pain and vulnerability inside. As she vanished round the corner, Blake felt the prickle of eyes on his back and he turned, scanning the road for anyone watching. A dark-blue saloon car with tinted windows pulled away from the curb just a few meters away, and Blake watched it go, an eerie sense of eyes on him as it passed.

He shook his head, the paranoia surely a hangover from the visions. He had to finish the Timotheus report, but he didn't want to go back to work now. It was time to face the past.

CHAPTER 6

BLAKE GOT OFF THE bus at the end of the lane, shivering a little in his thin jacket. Once he'd finally made the decision to come, he had left London as fast as possible and he hadn't brought his thicker coat. It was too much of a temptation to stay at home and avoid the confrontation he had feared for much of his adult life, the memory of his father looming large. Every mile he had come closer to arriving, every stop the bus had made, he had wanted to run back to London. But the room he had seen his father in through the watch haunted his thoughts, and he had to see what was really happening.

The little village of Long Farnborough was on the edge of the New Forest National Park, a train ride and then a bus from London, far enough to make it hard to visit without a car. It might well have been the other side of the world for how much he had seen his parents over the years. Blake walked slowly up the lane, the heavy weight of the past making his steps cumbersome. The scars on his hands throbbed, with cold perhaps, or with the memory of pain inflicted here.

Blake breathed in deeply, becoming more aware of the woodland around him as the birch and oak trees canopied above. Living in the city for so long, he had almost forgotten the clean scent of the forest, the ambient noise of birdsong and the rustling of woodland animals. The New Forest was actually one of the oldest forests in England, dense with whispers of the past, an echo of times when people lived closer to the earth. The intrepid walker, leaving the footpaths, could come upon an ancient monument or a round barrow from the early Bronze Age. In the past, Blake had tried to read some of the stones and trees around the burial sites, his hands flat against the rough surfaces, but he couldn't pick up any trace of those who had walked here.

One last corner. Blake steeled himself as he rounded it and saw the house his father had built with his own hands, the home he had walked away from. The place was simple, as befitted a man of God, and Blake knew his father had never cared much for the physical world, preferring to fix his eyes on Heaven. The red kitchen curtains were open and suddenly Blake saw his mother's face, his heart leaping in recognition. Precious Olofsson had married young, star struck by the prophet's dominance, and her features were still youthful, her black skin smooth. The lines around her eyes were deeper now, and she was still beautiful. Blake saw her smile light her face as she saw him and he almost wept, for there was no recrimination in her eyes, only love and welcome. *The prodigal son returns indeed*, he thought, walking faster to the door as it opened, and there she was.

"Daniel," she said, her voice soft and warm, like the bread she used to bake on a Saturday, when he would shape the dough into silly animals to make her laugh. Precious held her arms out and Blake walked into them, enfolding her.

"Oh, Mum," he whispered, eyes closed, feeling the prick of tears. Blake dwarfed her now, and he could feel how thin she was, how brittle. How vulnerable. Yet she stroked his back, her strength calming him.

"It's OK," she said, her breath warm on his neck. "I know why you've stayed away. But you're here now, and that's all that matters." She pulled away from him, clutching his hands, stroking the gloves as if she caressed the scars underneath. Her eyes shone with tears. "He's worse, you need to see him. The Lord will take him when He's ready, I know that, but the going is difficult."

Blake envied his mother's faith, an almost fatalistic view of the world. It meant she had believed his gift was God's will, but that his father's punishment was also meant to be. Perhaps it made life simpler to accept that, but Blake believed in being the author of one's own fate.

The sound of chanting came from the upstairs bedroom, rising to a crescendo and then a stream of voices praying in tongues. To some, it was the language of angels and to others, merely the expression of emotion through the vocalization of a meaningless dialect, a babble of incoherence made holy by belief.

"The Elders are with him," Precious said, her eyes shadowing. Blake tightened his arm around her. He knew how little the cabal of male Elders thought of the women in their congregation. Patriarchy was certainly alive and well in this community, a breakaway fundamentalist sect. His heart thumped at the thought of seeing the men, remembering how they had beaten him and others, how he had seen their abuse, and, God forgive him, he had never reported it.

"They shouldn't be too much longer." Precious sighed, shaking her head. "They've been interceding with God for nearly two hours. But if the Lord is calling your father, then who are we to try and keep him here? Heaven is a better place, and we must all long for the time when we will join our Savior."

Blake ignored the sense that he should answer her unspoken question. He had lost his faith a long time ago, and could no longer remember whether it was his father he had worshipped, or God himself. There seemed no difference in his childhood memories of the prophet leading the church in prayer, his deep voice extolling sermons that would leave the congregation on their knees, gasping for forgiveness.

The prayers stopped and after a moment, the Elders emerged at the top of the stairs, their voices hushed, faces grim. Blake's apprehension diminished as he noticed how much they had all aged. They had paunches, their faces sagged, and as much as they touted the poverty of faith, there was evidence of too much good living in their soft bodies. Blake stood taller, looking up at them.

Elder Paul Lemington saw him first, falling silent as the rest of the group followed his gaze.

"Daniel," Paul said as he walked down the stairs, eyes fixed on Blake. "It's been a long time."

Blake nodded, meeting the Elder's eyes, his gaze unflinching. He had nothing to fear from this man anymore, and looking at him now, Blake wondered how he could ever have been afraid of him. At the bottom of the stairs, Paul held out his hand. Blake looked at it for a moment, wanting to turn away but sensing his mother's eagerness for reconciliation.

After a moment, he held out his gloved hand to shake it. Paul glanced down and his pallor whitened a little, confronted by the evidence of his own past sin. How much did these men remember of what they had done to him? Blake wondered. How much did they still inflict on others? Blake pushed the thoughts aside as the Elders filed past him out into the dusk. It was time to face the man he'd been running from for years.

"I'll put the kettle on," Precious said. "And bring you up some tea." She pushed Blake gently towards the stairs. "Go on up to him now. He's in the spare room so I can hear him more easily."

The staircase loomed above him, like the ladder of Jacob ascending into Heaven, with his father enthroned at its height. Blake shook his head, remembering the shifting black creatures on the walls of the room above. There was no

Heaven here, only his own memories to confront. He trod the first stair and strength rose within him, pushing him up the rest.

At the top, Blake turned into the bedroom, pushing the door open as the bleep of medical machines beat time with his father's heart. The walls were a faded lilac, the same as they had been when he had left years ago, and the room was dominated by a double bed. His father lay curled, eyes closed, one side of his body tightened and hunched, pulling everything towards his center. The covers were twisted around him and saliva dripped from his mouth onto the pillow. Beads of sweat stood out on his forehead, evidence of a fever or perhaps the exertion of prayer.

Blake looked down at his father and felt a strange absence, as the pent-up anxiety left him. This wasn't the man he had left behind and feared beyond all else. Magnus Olofsson, the prophet of New Jerusalem Church, had now been reduced to this pitiful state. Sitting down next to the bed, Blake looked around the room. The vision he had seen of the black creatures on rotting walls came from this spot, he was sure of it, and yet, the room smelled of antiseptic and he could sense nothing wrong here. Perhaps the visions had been corrupted by his own emotional baggage, or perhaps the Elders had truly exorcised the room, cleansing it with their prayers.

"Unnng, unngh." The noise came from Magnus and Blake looked down into his father's eyes, the brilliant blue undimmed by the destruction of his physical body. There was defiance there, an attempt at strength even from that prone position. Blake remembered the blaze in them, blood dripping from the strap on the day he had run.

"I'm here, Dad," he said, his face taut, holding emotion in check. "I've come back."

Blake felt an overwhelming desire to put his hand over the prophet's eyes, to stop the judging gaze that was fixed on him. It wouldn't take much to pick up one of the pillows and hold it over the man's face, smothering him, taking him to the arms of his God that much faster. It would be a blessing, for Magnus Olofsson's Nordic heritage was battle born, where a good death was to die fighting, with a sword in your hand, cursing the heathen.

Instead, Blake picked up the Bible by the bed, his gloved hands running over the leather-bound book, pages edged with gold. A bookmark lay within, marking the place his mother was reading from. It opened at Psalm 55, and Blake read aloud from the page.

"'Let death steal over them; let them go down to Sheol alive; for evil is in their dwelling place and in their heart …'"

Blake's voice trailed off and he looked at the walls again, trying to imagine the creatures squatting there, drawing ever closer to feed, when Magnus finally crossed over to their realm. He had seen the largest one uncurl just above the old fireplace in his vision, but now there was nothing there but a basket of dried flowers.

"I still see the visions, Dad," Blake whispered. "You never managed to beat them out of me."

"Nnnngg." An utterance of protest. Blake looked down at his father again and saw something there. Was it regret, or was that what he wanted to see?

"When I touched your watch, I saw this room through your eyes, through your emotions. I saw something here, Dad … Dark creatures."

Magnus was silent, but his eyes went to the exact spot on the wall where Blake had seen the beast curled, shifting as it waited for the end. His father's breath became ragged, as if fear compacted his chest even more than the stroke had. Blake reached for his hand, and squeezed it. He felt a return of pressure, only faint, but it was still there.

"I want to try and see them again," Blake said. "I don't understand it, but I want to see what you do. Just put your hand on the Bible and I'll try to read you through it."

Magnus moaned, his eyes frightened, as if allowing Blake to see his visions would invite Satan back in by the acknowledgement of his gift. But he was clearly desperate, because he shifted his hand a little towards the book in acquiescence. Blake lifted his father's hand onto the Bible and then took off his gloves. Magnus' eyes fell on the scars, the ivory lines a pattern of his abuse, but there was no regret there, no apology.

Blake touched the Bible and a veil fell over the room as he sifted the emotions on the book for a sense of his father's present state. The strands solidified and Blake watched the walls shimmer, shift and darken until the lilac was gone, covered only with creatures of shadow. There were more than he had seen when he had read the watch. Now they clustered on the floor as well, some slithering over each other, snake-like, leaving slick oily patches behind them. Blake lifted his feet as he felt a movement under the bed, taking a sharp breath in fright. He didn't dare bend to look, instead turning to his father.

Blake moaned, his hand almost lifting from the book in horror at what he saw.

CHAPTER 7

JAMIE PULLED UP INTO the quiet street. The bike was her sanctuary, but it had the added benefit of making her journey through the winding streets of London a lot faster. As she dismounted and pulled off her protective gear, Jamie realized she was fully engaged with this case. For the first time in months, she could feel that spark of enthusiasm, her mind processing details, eager to discover more about the key people of interest. Missinghall had remained back at the station, pursuing the leads on some of the others, while she had come to see Petra Bennett. Jamie rang the bell on the basement flat, taking out her warrant card as she heard footsteps inside and the door opened.

Petra Bennett's face had the curious look of a deep-water fish: all lips and heavy cheeks, her body drooped as if gravity pulled more heavily on her than others. But her eyes were a vivid blue, almost turquoise, and her face was alive with an inquisitive, watchful expression.

"Detective, come on in. The place is a bit chaotic as I've only just got back from the Fun Run. So much to do! But I've just made coffee if you'd like some."

"That would be great, thanks."

Jamie followed Petra into the small downstairs flat. Boxes were piled up in one corner, bunting and banners in green and gold spilling from the top. There were two large photographic canvases on the wall flanking a fireplace in an otherwise sparse room. The canvases depicted stone sculptures, rocks piled high into towers that seemed to perch like miracles on the edge of the sea. One spiraled into itself, a multi-hued grey, and the other reached to the heavens with almost impossible balance.

"What is it you do, Ms Bennett?"

"Oh, please call me Petra," she said, pouring black coffee from a percolator into a bright red mug and handing it to Jamie. "I teach Spanish to private students. Business Spanish, and some conversation. But I'm also an artist." Petra gestured at the canvases. "These are my offerings to the gods of the sea, temporary sculptures on the edge of the tide. Even with these photographs, I fear I take too much of their power. They're meant to be ephemeral, lost almost as soon as they're completed." Petra held her head to one side, gazing into the frames. "Stone is the earth's gift to us, and perhaps our ancestors were right to believe they hold the partial spirits of Gaia. When we hew them apart, when we take them for our own and shape them to our purposes, they become husks with no power, only aesthetic."

"They're beautiful," Jamie said, trying to read the complex emotion held on the horizon of blue and grey.

"I write my confessions in stone, Detective. But they're not to be understood by all."

"And what do you have to confess?" Jamie asked, eyebrows arching at the words.

Petra shook her head, her mouth twisting into something that could have been a smile.

"My own obsessions perhaps, but certainly not the crime you're here to investigate."

Jamie turned to look at the room, as she waited for Petra to speak into the silence. Pebbles of all sizes were piled in plastic boxes in one corner. Some had shapes carved into the surface, others were painted in the contours of the stone, all smooth with rounded curves.

"I've collected those from beaches all over the world," Petra said. "The figures on them represent the journeys I've taken, or those that others have traveled."

Jamie remembered walking along Lyme Regis beach with Polly, telling her stories of the dinosaurs that had once lived there, the ancient bodies that were crushed and preserved within the rock strata. Polly had been fascinated, picking up the stones to examine them for fossilized remains. She had been in a lot of pain from motor neurone disease by then, but she had remained deeply curious about the world around her. Jamie's chest tightened at the precious memory of the time with her daughter, now locked in the past.

"Most people will pick up stones when they walk along a beach," Petra continued, her voice mesmerizing. "It's a human fascination. Pebbles fit within the palm and their touch is an element we crave. My interest started when my Gran used to paint flowers on the stones she found on the beach when I visited each summer. It gave me something to watch, and then to learn, and now I create them for others."

Petra's eyes were fathomless, like the places close to land where the continental shelf dropped off to the deepest parts of the ocean. She was at once unknowable depths and light waters in the shallows. Jamie felt the woman was somehow wiser than her years – an old soul – but wisdom didn't necessarily prevent murderous rage.

"Stone is the medium that calls to me," Petra said. "Its reputation is to be hard hearted, grey and strong, building cathedrals that last for generations. But stone can be smoothed by water, its surface rubbed into something else. That same stone can be decorative, or used as a weapon, for each stone has its own message. Once I discern it, then I paint. Sometimes the message just calls to me." Petra bent to the pile and held out a small grey stone when she straightened. "Here, Detective. I think this one is for you."

Jamie couldn't help but reach for the stone, something compelling her to take it. A tiny dancer spun alone, the folds of her dress artfully rendered in just a few strokes of black paint, her passion contained within the frozen moment. Thoughts of the tango *milonga* flashed through Jamie's mind, a passion she had developed as Polly had become sicker as a way of sublimating pain and grief into the intensity of dance. Petra couldn't possibly know of this secret interest: it wasn't something she shared with work colleagues, and she even used a different name. She hadn't been to tango since Polly's death, as the thought of celebrating physical movement seemed sacrilegious. Perhaps it was time to return. Jamie held out the stone.

"Thank you for the kind thought," she said, handing it back. "But I can't take anything from you, even as a gift. As my colleague told you on the phone, I'm here as part of the investigation into the murder of Dr Christian Monro."

Petra sighed and her eyes darkened as she took back the pebble. "I can't say I'm surprised at his death. He was superior and condescending, treating patients as evidence for his pet theories. But I also needed him and his ... special brand of therapy. The man was a bastard, but he was actually helping me break through some of my own creative blocks."

"Did he handle your medication?" Jamie asked, thinking of the drugs in the large cupboard.

Petra shook her head. "I'm not on medication, Detective. I don't ascribe to the labels of mental illness or the drugs the establishment tries to control us with. That's why I work with Psyche. Some may say that I have a form of depression, but I just call it life. It's those people who look at the world and don't feel overwhelmed sometimes that I worry for. There's so much darkness, isn't it natural to retreat into despair sometimes?"

Jamie thought of the pills in her own bathroom cabinet,

and how she counted them out every day, holding that deadly dosage in her hand before counting them back into the bottle. She understood the pull of oblivion all too well.

"Did you know of the room behind Monro's main office?" Jamie asked.

Petra smiled, her eyes flashing with memories that clearly gave her pleasure.

"Yes, and I went there willingly, Detective." Her tone was unapologetic. "You have to understand that some of us need restraint in order to find true freedom. In temporal pain, there is a release of pressure, a way to keep the desire for more harm at bay. Monro understood that, although sometimes I think he studied us as aberrations."

"Us?"

"Yes, of course there were others. We saw each other in the waiting area sometimes, and there were men as well as women. I don't even think it was sexual for Monro, he really did believe in restraint and punishment as an efficacious treatment for mental illness. Perhaps we deviants proved some part of his pet theory. But, let's face it, if you start offering spanking and physical relief as part of your therapy, then word will get around and certain types of people will seek it out."

Jamie raised an eyebrow. "It seems an unusual form of therapy for a psychiatrist."

"Humans are unusual, don't you think?" Petra indicated the pile of painted stones. "Each one of these is similar in some ways and totally different in others. What one person thinks is strange, another embraces. The problem with society is judgement, so much of what is experienced stays underground and repressed. Shame is another form of repression, of course, one our society excels in, and those of us labeled as mentally ill are particularly aware of that."

"Do you think others who went to him were ashamed of what they did?"

"Perhaps." Petra nodded. "But there have been many therapists who strayed into the physical realm. The great Carl Jung was rumored to have had an affair with a young client, Sabina Spielrein, and she admitted in her letters to being aroused by beatings from her father. Some think that became the basis of her sexual relationship with Jung. And, of course, the vibrator was invented by doctors in the Victorian era whose arms were tired from manually stimulating women as part of treatment for hysteria."

Jamie made a couple more notes to follow up.

"But surely Monro must have kept that aspect of his practice secret and for select patients only, so how did you find out about him?"

"Through another client of his, Lyssa Osborne," Petra said. "Of course, I know Matthew Osborne through Psyche, he's just amazing, tireless in his campaigning. I've known him a number of years, even before he was an MP. But I actually met Lyssa for the first time at a life drawing class, or should I say, death drawing, because the models were posed as corpses." Jamie raised an eyebrow and Petra smiled. "Macabre, yes, but a new way to look at the body. Lyssa was brilliant at everything she did and the lines on her paper evoked a sensuality in death that I couldn't capture on my page."

Petra's eyes focused on a point beyond the stone gateway on the wall. "In the end I just watched her sketch, the curve of the woman's breasts, the darkness between her thighs, the way Lyssa licked her lips as if she would devour what she saw. We had a drink afterwards and she told me that she was in love with death and she was seeing a psychiatrist to try and fall out of love with it, to reconnect with her physical self." Petra paused, her voice quieter now. "I too find myself drawn to death, to die perhaps like Virginia Woolf, weighed down with my own painted stones in my pockets. Monro had ways of sublimating those desires and after our sessions,

I was renewed and could go another week without wanting to rush into death's embrace. Perhaps you may call his treatment some kind of perversion or abuse of trust, but I didn't wish him dead, Detective. In fact, his death brings my own that much closer." Petra laughed, a brittle sound with little joy in it. "'Beneath it all, desire for oblivion runs.' That's from Philip Larkin. Poets always say it best, don't they?"

There was no trace of concern in Petra's voice at the talk of suicide. Once Jamie would have been shocked, even appalled at the woman's words, but now she understood. Every day she woke alone in the flat without Polly, she wanted to take that one last step into oblivion. It wasn't hard to die, it was only hard to live.

"Do you know of anyone who wanted Monro dead or who threatened him in any way?" Jamie asked.

Petra fell silent for a moment, biting her lip a little.

"He would talk of suicide as the ultimate control," she said, "as the moment when you exercise the last freedom any of us have in this life. But he would also caution not to use that power lightly, for once it's used, it's finished and spent, the power is gone. For someone to murder him, it would be to take that ultimate power of choice away. He wasn't allowed to meet death on his own terms, and that would have been torture for him. But no, I can't think of anyone specifically."

"Can I ask where you were last night?" Jamie asked.

"Of course. I was here, Detective. Alone with my stones." Petra smiled. "I have no alibi, but then I really have no motive, either."

CHAPTER 8

Blake blinked, desperate to believe the vision was wrong, but he could still see it. A creature was curled around his father's back, its spines embedded in the old skin, piercing through the thin gown, the visage lizard-like and darkly scaled. Its tongue darted out, licking at Magnus' cheek, tasting the sweat there. This thing would be the first to feed. Blake met his father's eyes, and comprehension darted between them. He knew then that this was the world his father had always perceived and that Blake had only glimpsed the edges of.

"Daniel, Daniel, stop!"

His mother's voice intruded into the trance and Precious pushed his shoulder, jerking Blake's hand away from the Bible.

"You know he hates your visions," she said, almost in tears as she bent to brush damp hair from Magnus' brow. "How could you do it here with him?"

Blake put his glove back on, looking around the lilac room, his eyes lingering on the walls and then back at his father's form on the bed. He could no longer perceive the creatures, and there was no sense of anything evil here. Was it just a hallucination, an extension of his father's belief that there were demons in the world waiting to feed on dying souls? Or was there some kind of supernatural reality that he had glimpsed through the eyes of a man of faith. In nearly twenty years of visions, Blake had never seen this before.

He frowned, brow furrowed as he walked around the bed to stand behind his father. He reached down and patted the bed where the creature had been curled. Nothing. He held his hand in the space behind Magnus' neck, thinking perhaps he could feel something, like a patch of disturbed air. But it was more likely the breeze from the window, open to let fresh air into this room of sickness.

"I know it's a shock seeing him like this," Precious said. "I'm so sorry I didn't send for you earlier." She sighed. "I didn't think the years would pass so fast, and look at you now." She held out a hand across Magnus' body and Blake took it, squeezing a little. The least he could do was comfort her for a moment, but he couldn't tell her of what he had seen in this room. He looked down and caught sight of a black mark on his father's back. Could this be evidence of the creature?

Blake pulled away the gown that was tied at the back of his father's neck. A moan of protest made him pull his hand away in remembrance of what the man would have done for such trespass in stronger days. He had never seen his father less than fully clothed.

"It's OK, Dad," Blake said, knowing he needed to see what it was. "I just want to look at the mark."

"It's a tattoo," Precious said, her voice strangely dull. "He would never tell me what it meant, but he has had it since I met him. He would get angry if I asked about it."

The symbol began at the very top of Magnus' spine, just below his neck, and as Blake parted the gown, he could see it spread over the main part of his father's back. The ink was faded but there was clearly a design of triple claws, overlaying each other in a knot. The thick lines were bisected with scars and welts in a rhythmic pattern, always the same diagonal down from each shoulder. It seemed his father had beaten himself as well as his son over the years, atoning for whatever sin this tattoo represented. A glimmer of understanding for the man flickered through Blake's mind. He pulled the edges of the gown up and tucked in the covers again, placing his hand on his father's hunched shoulder and tightening his fingers a little, the pressure as close to a gesture of love as he could manage. Blake's own scars were as deep as the ones on his father's back, and neither set would ever fully heal now. But there had to be something in his father's past that would explain the creatures that lurked here waiting to feed.

"How did you meet each other, Mum? You've never told me."

Precious smiled, her eyes shining, and Blake envied the simple pleasure of that memory of young love, so far from his own drunken one-night stands. His thoughts flickered to Jamie: of what could possibly be if they could face their pain together.

"It was back in London," Precious said. "I had just started college and my Pentecostal congregation in Brixton had a visiting preacher." She reached down to stroke Magnus' hair as she spoke. "Your father was a magnificent servant of God and when he spoke, I felt his words go straight to my heart. He stayed in London and soon after, we started dating, with chaperones of course. I know there have been hard times, Daniel, but you were born of love and of God."

Blake nodded. "And what about before that? Where did he live before London?"

"His family are from the very north of Sweden, almost on the border of the fjords of Norway. But he would never say any more than that, and we've never been to visit." She paused, looking down at her husband. "I don't even know their names, and that's how he wanted it. He needed to forget the past, whatever it was, and I honored that. I expect you to as well."

"But I need to know more," Blake said. "It's important, Mum. I saw something ... I can't explain, but I think Dad needs help."

Magnus moaned again, his words unintelligible, but his tone made Precious pale and Blake recognized the man's hold over her. She exhaled.

"So be it. Come, I'll show you the chest."

She picked up the Bible and walked to the door. With a last glance at his father's pale face, Blake followed Precious out the room and up the stairs towards his parents' bedroom. It had been out of bounds when he had lived here, a child's gate and later a beating keeping him away from their private space. But he had often sneaked in when they were out and he knew the huge window looked out into the forest, the bed facing the green expanse. How often had his father lain there and thought of the wilds of Sweden and the forests of his own youth?

"It's underneath the bed," Precious said, a waver in her voice. "He would never let me touch it. Even to clean. The only time he ever beat me properly was when I tried to move it." Her eyes darted to Blake's. "I know that's no comfort to you, but the nights after he beat you, he would cry in my arms. He was terribly afraid of something, Daniel. Something that he thought might come for you."

Blake knelt down, pulled the covers up and looked under the bed. A small chest sat under the side his father had slept in, the dull wood sucking in the light and deepening the surrounding shadows. He reached under and pulled it out. A thick padlock held the chest closed and the metal was rusty, clearly not opened for many years.

"He kept the key in here," Precious said, placing the Bible on top of the bed. "That's how much it means to him, for this book has been within arm's reach as long as I've known him. Even when we met it was already worn with use. I discovered the key once, years ago when we were first married ..." Her hand went to her cheek, eyes glazing over at the memory. "But I learned quickly not to pry into his past."

Blake's anger flared at her obvious remembrance of violence, but the past was done now, and all they had left was the broken man in the bed downstairs. Precious turned to the back of the Bible. A small envelope was taped to the inside of the cover, a handwritten verse on one side. Deuteronomy 28:48.

"'In hunger and thirst,'" Precious recited from memory, "'in nakedness and dire poverty, you will serve the enemies the Lord sends against you. He will put an iron yoke on your neck until he has destroyed you …' I've pondered this many times over the years. Why link that particular verse to the key?"

She slipped the key from the envelope and handed it to Blake. He pushed it into the padlock and with a few wiggles, it finally twisted and the lock opened. He pulled it off the box and laid it down by the side as Precious knelt next to him, her breath shallow, expectant.

Blake lifted the lid, tugging a little to free the hinges. Inside was another layer of wrapping, this time a kind of oilcloth, like the type found on sailboats. It must have been cream colored once, but was now a dirty ivory. Blake tipped the chest a little and the object fell out into his gloved hand. He laid it on the floor and pulled apart the sailcloth, revealing a book bound in deep burgundy leather. A symbol was inscribed on the front, a circle in the center, bisected by four lines with prongs on either end. The lines were cross-hatched with other markings, the whole image giving the impression of a twisted snowflake.

"It's beautiful," Precious said, reaching out a fingertip to touch the leather. "But why keep this hidden?"

Blake lifted the book from its covering and opened it.

"Galdrabók," he read from the first page, flicking through the heavy book. "It looks like Swedish or some kind of

Nordic language, and look at these diagrams and pictures."

"Oh, Lord," Precious whispered. "It's a book of some kind of magic, isn't it?"

Blake's fingers itched, wanting to take off his gloves and touch the book, read the chest, to see what his father was hiding in his past. But he couldn't do it with his mother there.

"I need to know more about it, Mum. Clearly it's important to Dad, but he can't tell us why. Go back down to him, and I'll check it out on the internet."

"It shouldn't even be in the house." Precious stood, her face furrowed with concern. "Leviticus 20, verse 6. 'If a person turns to mediums and necromancers, I will set my face against that person and will cut him off from amongst his people.' Goodness, what did your father do?"

She walked out the door, her footsteps heavy as she went back downstairs. Blake could hear her whispered prayers, interceding for Magnus with her Lord, and for a moment, he was envious of her certain faith. He turned the pages of the book carefully, and within its thin paper, he found a folded chart written in burgundy ink. Blake spread it open on the floor to find a genealogical history of the last few generations of the Olofsson family, written in Swedish. There were strange etchings next to some of the names, runes that marked out individuals in each generation. The symbol lay next to his own name, and that of his father and grandfather. Blake frowned. He needed to understand what this book was.

Laying it down, he took off his gloves and used his smartphone to access the internet, wanting to know more before he tried to tap into the visions. He found a reference quickly. The Galdrabók grimoire was a book of Icelandic spells with invocations to Christian saints, demons and the old Norse gods, as well as instructions for the use of herbs and other magical items. The text was a mixture of Latin, runic script, sacred images and Icelandic magic sigils, symbols of power. What was his father doing with such a text? The only way to find out was to see what visions the book could release to him. Taking a deep breath, Blake laid his bare hands on the leather.

the way I was thinking with, the weight I finally was
to find out was to see what was in there I would spend a whole
picture spending myself. Maybe half the time I was at
the mill or

CHAPTER 9

Chadwick Street was tucked into the warren of residences and government buildings on the edge of Westminster, walking distance to Millbank and the Houses of Parliament. The building was painted in shades of cinnamon and cream, with shutters around the windows giving a slightly Mediterranean feel to this bureaucratic hub of the capital. Taking off her leather protective gear, Jamie pulled a black jacket from her pannier and straightened her clothes. She redid her tight bun, winding her black hair and securing it with a clip, tucking in the stray ends. But the transformation into professionalism was wearing thin these days and the bike felt more like her real self than the buttoned-up Detective. The fragmentation of her world was seeping into the job, and part of Jamie craved a final collapse. She rang the bell.

Matthew Osborne pulled the door open within a few seconds, clearly having heard her bike arrive. He was freshly showered, his hair still wet, and he smelled of pine forests after rain. With blue jeans and a black shirt open at the neck and rolled up sleeves, he looked like he had stepped out of a weekend magazine advertising the good life of the rich and famous.

"Detective, come on in. I'm Matthew." He held out his

hand and Jamie shook it. His grip was firm, fingers smooth against her skin, and she noticed the slightly crooked tooth in his otherwise perfect smile. It was a chink of normality in his media-constructed image, but perhaps even that was designed. "I'll put the kettle on, and then we can have a chat about what you need."

"Thank you." Jamie followed Matthew inside, shutting the door behind her. She glanced around the flat as she walked into a large living space, leading to a small kitchen. The room was furnished in shades of champagne, a muted undertone, with furniture that looked comfortable but still expensive. The outstanding element was a feature wall with stripes of fuchsia, lemon and vermilion, hung with stunning pieces of modern art. In one, a woman's hand and the side of her head emerged from the canvas, as if she was trying to climb out of the wall behind. Another was a riot of color over a black tangle of what looked like neurons in the brain. It should have been chaotic, but there was a space in the middle of the pandemonium, an opening for calm.

"My sister, Lyssa, was very talented," Matthew said, emerging from the kitchen, his voice wistful. "These are just a couple from her portfolio. She could have gone so far with it, and creating the work calmed her, kept her from spiraling downwards." He paused, gazing at the woman's hand reaching out to him, as if she was calling for his help. The kettle whistled and he shook his head slightly, reverting to charm. "Now, how do you take your tea?"

"Black with one, please."

Matthew stirred in a sugar and brought it to Jamie in a blue mug with a chip in the rim. It made her almost smile to see that he was so clearly at home with imperfection. Perhaps there was more to this man than just the media profile.

"Now, what can I help you with?" Matthew asked, sitting on one of the chairs and indicating that Jamie should do the same.

"I'm investigating a homicide that occurred this morning at the Imperial War Museum."

Matthew's brow furrowed. "Surely not at our Fun Run? It went off without a hitch and all participants were accounted for."

Jamie shook her head. "No, actually, it was within the main building, unrelated to your event. But the victim was your sister's psychiatrist."

"That bastard Monro, are you sure?"

She caught a hint of satisfaction in Matthew's eyes.

"You sound pleased."

"I am. Not to speak ill of the dead, of course, but I believe his treatment only made Lyssa worse over time." Matthew looked intently at Jamie, but she could see no hint of his underlying thoughts. With so many years of hiding things, a politician was a real match for the police. "He tried her on so many drug regimes but she was afraid of needles and the experience was always terrifying. There was no spark left in her after dosage, the drugs emptied her and left her anemic and stale. As they began to wear off, she would fill that emptiness with ideas and thoughts and color, but the cyclic regime of years wore her down. Each time the colors came back, they were more muted, pastels instead of primary shades."

Matthew pointed at the walls. "As you can see, she hated pastels, Detective. She couldn't bear baby pink and duck-egg blue. She wanted strong bold shades, like her personality. You would have noticed her in a crowd." He pointed to a picture on the mantelpiece and Jamie stood for a better look. Lyssa had been strikingly handsome, not beautiful in a traditional sense but with strong features that drew the eyes. Her hair was cropped short and dyed a deep red, and she had tattooed eyebrows in a Celtic design. Jamie felt Matthew's analytical gaze take in her own black work-wraith uniform, her dark hair in a tight bun, her colorless skin. She suddenly felt tepid compared to this woman whose eyes were so vibrant and whose photo exuded life. Jamie felt an edge of that passion in tango, but it had become a secret part of her fractured life these days. She sat back down as Matthew continued.

"We're all coerced into uniformity but Lyssa never gave into it. Despite our lip service to diversity, society wants conformity. We frown at the misbehavior of others. That's the real reason that Lyssa was medicated ... so she couldn't be remarkable. You might think the inhuman restraint, the physical violence done to the mad is over, Detective, but the restraint has just moved from the outside to the inside, and the drugs are just a replacement for the manacles of Bedlam. Perhaps the drugs were worse because they left Lyssa without the freedom of her mind."

Jamie thought of Polly in the last days before her death, surfing the internet and learning new things, desperate to suck everything she could from life. Her body had been twisted and malfunctioning, but her mind remained clear and curious until the end.

"I'm sorry for your loss," Jamie said. She had spoken those words many times over the years, but now she actually understood them deep within. "But without the drugs, surely Lyssa may have ended up self-harming even more. Perhaps the chemical restraint helped in some way."

There was a flash in Matthew's eyes, something Jamie couldn't quite identify. He tamped it down quickly, returning his face to the politician's equilibrium.

"That's the opinion of many, for sure." His words were curt, ending that thread of conversation. "Now what exactly can I help you with, Detective?"

"I need to know where you were last night."

Matthew grinned, the charming smile that housewives all over the nation doted on.

"Oh, I'm a suspect. That's a new one."

"Not a suspect as such. I'm just following up on leads

from the workplace of the deceased, and of course, you were at the museum this morning."

Matthew nodded. "Of course, it's no trouble and I'm always happy to help the police with enquiries." He took a sip of tea. "This morning I arrived at the site early, around nine, but I wasn't the first, and I wasn't anywhere near the main museum. I parked on Lambeth Walk near the London Eye Hostel, which I'm sure you can check. Last night I was out to dinner with a fellow MP. She'll certainly support that. We parted ways at around ten-thirty and I was tucked up in bed by eleven. But I do live alone, Detective, and despite what the press may speculate about my love life, I actually live a quiet, private existence. You won't find scandal here. Lyssa lived with me for a time ... but of course, she can no longer speak on my behalf."

Jamie could hear the grief in his voice, and a tinge of guilt at his sister's death. She had thought life would be impossible without Polly to come home to, so perhaps Matthew Osborne felt the same. He had constructed a life that was impenetrable because of his grief, and Jamie knew she pushed others aside when they tried to come closer. She thought of Blake Daniel, and how she kept him at arm's length. Was this how Matthew Osborne behaved, too?

"I'd like to know more about Psyche," she said. "What do you want to achieve with the charity?"

"An end to the stereotypes," Matthew replied. "An admission that madness is a spectrum and we're all on it somewhere. No more us and them, just a continuum of the amazing human mind with all its complexity. We can't do a blood test and say for sure whether someone is crazy, and we can only diagnose Alzheimer's accurately after death. So is madness in the physical brain or all in the existential mind? And where is the line crossed?"

Matthew's eyes shone with passion and he clenched his fist as he spoke, clearly used to engaging hostile opponents in the political arena.

"Does Lyssa's experience drive your campaign?" Jamie asked, watching him soften a little at his sister's name.

Matthew nodded. "She started suffering a mood disorder in her teens, and I was always her champion big brother." He tapped his front tooth with an elegant fingernail. "This crooked one is the result of a brawl defending her against school bullies. I keep it unfixed as a reminder of the intolerance that the mentally ill suffer at the hands of those who don't understand them. Psyche has developed over time, an attempt to take this beyond one individual, and as Secretary of State for Health, I'm in a prime position to make the so-called mad my life's work."

"Is the word mad appropriate?" Jamie asked, wondering at the stigma of its use.

Matthew smiled. "Oh, yes. These days language is reclaimed. I support a less extreme viewpoint, but Lyssa was a member of Mad Pride, focused on taking control of madness and accepting it. The prison others build can become a fortress of strength. For that reason, Lyssa always loved the Tower of London, with all of its mad connotations. We used to stand on the arches of Tower Bridge looking down into it when we first moved here." Matthew's voice was wistful with memories of happier times. He stood and walked to the artwork on the wall, staring at it as he spoke, as if he saw beyond it to other realities. "Madness is not an aberration, Detective. It's not abnormal. It's just part of the spectrum of the human condition. Most hide their little crazy moments, but they happen to us all." Jamie's thoughts flashed once more to the pills in her medicine cabinet.

"And, of course," Matthew continued, "without the mad, Shakespeare would be without his tragic heroes who teach us so much. Surely Hamlet was clinically depressed, Ophelia to the point of suicide, and of course, there's demented Lear, howling against the storm with Tom of Bedlam for company as he raved against his daughters. The way families treat the mad is perhaps part of the truth of Lear. And look at Macbeth. Surely there was a hint of paranoia in his murderous behavior?"

"But don't some people really need help?" Jamie said. "The world is hard enough to manage for people in full possession of their faculties. The forms we have to fill in, the bureaucracy, the rules we have to obey to live in society. These must be difficult things for people whose reality is skewed."

"But who's to say that their reality is any less valid than our own?" Matthew asked.

"I guess the government, the police, the rules of our society say that a certain reality must be upheld."

Matthew threw his hands up with exasperation. "But look at this world. Every day, we hear of human depravity on the news. Of parents beating and starving their children, of countries spying and stealing secrets, of torture, mass murder, incoming disasters both natural and manmade. This keeps people on the edge of their own madness, controlled by fear of what may come if they don't obey. Surely this is why we are so medicated? The number of people on prescription drugs for anxiety and depression is out of control. Our society is wrecked, for 'those who the Gods wish to destroy, first they make mad.'"

Jamie raised a questioning eyebrow.

"Attributed to an anonymous source or sometimes Euripides," Matthew said. "The Greek tragedies were filled with the mad. My sister was delighted when she found out that Lyssa was the goddess of frenzied madness. She had been known by the name Mel all our childhood, but she embraced the name Lyssa after she studied Greek myth. I'm not sure what came first, her name or the madness that took her.

"You're right, though. Lyssa was medicated because her

mania took her to the edge of danger, and her depression took her over it." Matthew ran a finger gently down the curve of the woman's arm as she emerged from the artwork. Jamie could almost feel his touch on her own skin. "She walked the line successfully for so many years, but then, of course, she went over the edge. On the drugs she tottered like an old woman along well-worn paths, panting and wheezing to achieve anything small. Without them, she ran and laughed and danced along the cliff's edge, creating masterpieces, but she was always in danger of falling."

Matthew spun back to look at Jamie, his voice impassioned. "But isn't it better to live your life like a comet, blazing across the sky, rather than suffering this dull bus ride of normality? Of course I wanted a lifetime with my sister, but not with the dull, medicated version. She wasn't Lyssa then – perhaps she was plain old Mel, the compliant, good child my parents always wanted. Like I am, perhaps, like all who subscribe to the normal and expected way of life. But aren't the mad, the crazy, actually the ones who work at a job they hate, with people they can't stand, digging themselves deeper into debt, medicating themselves daily with food and TV and alcohol? Who's to say that isn't the more damaging way to live?"

Matthew's eyes met Jamie's, his gaze penetrating.

"Let's be honest, Detective, you don't look well. As someone who's lived alongside depression, you exude its dark energy right now."

Jamie met his eyes as she took another sip of tea. His suggestion disarmed her and his ability to see what she hid with a veneer of normality was uncanny. She wore no makeup to work, and her eyes were shadowed with dark rings. Her skin was too pale and she was too thin. Self-harming wasn't just for those diagnosed as mentally ill. She met Matthew's eyes.

"It's not your concern, but I do understand your perspective. I've lost someone too."

88

"And is grief a form of madness, Detective? In the DSM, the psychiatrist's manual for diagnostics, it only becomes depression after several months of suffering. Before that, grief is just grief, but then somehow it crosses some designated line and becomes something you can medicate away. I embrace it because it drives the passion for my work. When Lyssa was alive, I fought to claim her equal rights in the mind of society, and now she's dead, I work to establish the continuum of the mad and stop the abuses before they become too great.

"People forget that it was the Americans in the 1920s who started the enforced sterilization of the mentally ill based on the assumption of bad breeding. Hitler only followed their example, targeting the mentally ill before the Jews or gypsies. The mad were the first to be slaughtered, and there is still considerable prejudice against them. It wouldn't take much to tip people back into the old ways of thinking. I have my suspicions that Monro wasn't too far from those thoughts."

"What do you mean?" Jamie asked, noting how tense Matthew had become, his muscular frame taut. He paused for a moment, as if he was unsure whether to continue. "Please," she said. "It will help the investigation if you can tell us of Monro's political leanings."

Matthew nodded. "His name came up in a confidential paper distributed by RAIN. Do you know of them?"

Jamie noted it down. "No, but please go on."

"RAIN is a government agency associated with the Ministry of Defense, so it's not under my portfolio. It stands for Research into Advanced Intelligence Network, and their work is aimed at high-risk but high-payoff programs that have the potential to provide Britain with an overwhelming intelligence advantage against future adversaries. That's about all I know, despite trying to find out more. I did see a report on psychic ability and its correlation with mental health, and Monro was one of the names on it. But the agency is incredibly secretive and I couldn't find out anymore. Perhaps you can, Detective. Perhaps it's related to his murder."

Jamie remembered the raindrop symbol on some of Monro's files. It could be connected to RAIN somehow, but what exactly was Monro's involvement?

"It's ironic that RAIN are studying mental illness," Matthew continued, a dark smile in his voice. "There are studies that show that over half of us would meet the diagnostic criteria for mental disorder in our lifetimes. But we keep our thoughts to ourselves so no one will notice the throes of insanity. We maintain a semblance of normality, but who knows what violence goes on behind the closed curtains of our minds? After all, pills can now make us better than well. Why feel even slightly down if you can pop a pill and make it go away, live in happy la-la land, dulled to sensation? Why be even hurt a little when you can medicate to oblivion?"

Jamie thought of the ephedrine she used as uppers, about the sleeping pills she took to keep the nightmares at bay.

"And what do your parents think about your work?" she asked.

Matthew held his arms wide and took a little bow. "I'm their golden boy, Detective." His voice was mocking, bitter. "Their son is an MP, a respected member of the community, on the TV and in the papers. Lyssa was the more spectacular but also the more disappointing. They judged her to be wanting and took her to a psychiatrist in her early teens. She started the medication then. It was only with me that she felt safe enough to come off the drugs." He took another deep breath. "Is it just me, or are you also sick of being conformist? Why can't we all go a little crazy sometimes?"

"But suicide?" Jamie said. "Surely you don't support it."

"I support the right of an adult to take their own life if it's a considered decision. Think about it. Some days it's a surprise that we continue to live. It's much harder to keep getting up and living in this world than it is to give up and relax into the darkness. Embracing oblivion is just a choice, Detective."

"But the misery of those left behind," Jamie said. "Your own grief at Lyssa's death? Surely that would be better avoided? She could have created more, perhaps found happiness on another day."

Matthew ran his fingers along a crack that wound its way up from the fireplace to the ceiling. In any other house, it would have been plastered over, filled in and fixed. But here, it had been made a feature, and Jamie noticed the hands of tiny creatures emerging from the plaster, drawn in black ink. It was hard to tell whether they were imps from a dark place, or fairies coming forth with a blessing.

"Lyssa believed in embracing the cracks in our lives," Matthew said, his voice tinged with a sigh. "But her death was not such a simple thing."

"How did she …?"

"We rented a garage in the next street. I've never needed a car in London, but Lyssa loved to drive. It gave her a sense of freedom and escape. Sometimes she would drive to the ocean for the day, just to see the horizon in shades of blue. She loved the mad weather." Matthew laughed a little. "You know what I mean."

Jamie nodded, waiting for him to continue.

"She had been away the weekend before, some special retreat Monro had got her into, so I didn't see her much that week. The final day, she glammed up in her favorite dress and these brilliant red, Spanish flamenco heels. She loved them. She had a bottle of champagne and one of my crystal glasses with her. Only one, mind you, because she was always going to do it alone. She blocked the garage doors, making sure they were insulated, and then turned the ignition on. She took a couple of sleeping pills with the champagne … I imagine her toasting me." His voice trailed off for a moment.

"Eventually the exhaust fumes seeped out of the garage and someone reported it, but it was hours later. I was out, just another day on the job, campaigning for her rights, and those like her. She died of carbon monoxide poisoning. She just closed her eyes and fell asleep."

"I'm so sorry," Jamie said, his loss echoing within her, but there was also a tinge of anger. Lyssa had wasted a life, when Polly would gladly have seized that spark.

"She had always talked about suicide. It was one of our frequent discussions and she agreed to the medication in order to modulate her compulsions. But she missed her bolus injection appointment that week, and she didn't tell me." Matthew's head dropped to his hands. "She was my responsibility."

"She was an adult," Jamie said. "It was her choice."

"Oh, I don't begrudge her the choice to die. It's being left behind I resent."

Jamie wanted to tell him about Polly, wanted to tell him about the pills she had in her cabinet and the struggle every day not to take them. The faint glimmer of hope that she saw in a possible future even without the glue that held her life together.

"My sister was born special," Matthew said. "Her eyes rarely met ours as a baby, but instead, she smiled at beings in another realm. She could see through the veil of this reality, Detective. We are all given a spark of madness, but for her, it fanned into a flame and I helped it grow. We see such a poor version of this life but she could hold the whole world in her mind."

"But she couldn't stand it?"

Matthew shook his head. "The world implied she couldn't stand it. If I could have kept her protected, away from those like Monro who treated her as an invalid, she would have been safe. But they drugged her and she said it dulled her world and made her into one of us."

"One of us?"

"Those who walk in darkness and call it reality. But our reality wasn't worth living for, she said. If she couldn't fly with the angels, then why bother? In my opinion, it's not the mentally ill who are dangerous, it's those who control, medicate and abuse them."

Jamie sensed the undercurrent of animosity. Had that emotion spilled into violence?

"Did you know that Monro had some more – unusual – treatments as part of his practice?" she asked.

Matthew's eyes narrowed. He knew, for sure.

"I heard rumors that he had affairs with some of his patients, but Lyssa would never have been up for that. She certainly had no trouble with sex, Detective. When she was manic, she was irresistible." His words made Jamie wonder just how close the siblings had been.

"Did she have any papers or diaries?" Jamie asked.

"She wrote a diary in the months before her death," Matthew said, his voice tired. "I can't bear to read it, but perhaps it might offer some clues about Monro."

Jamie nodded. "If you can bear to part with it for a few days, I'll see what it contains."

Matthew stood and went to the bookcase. He pulled a red Moleskine notebook from the shelf.

"Be gentle with her memory."

In his words, Jamie heard the depths of his grief, and she felt an echo of her own for Polly. The sting of tears threatened and she stood to take the book from him.

"Of course, I'll take great care with it, and return it to you as soon as possible."

CHAPTER 10

A s B l a k e l a i d h i s hands on the Galdrabók, a rush of waters overlaid with the howling of wind filled his brain, yet he could see nothing but mist. He grasped for a tendril of emotional resonance in the haze and found only terror. Apprehensive, he followed the feeling with his mind and suddenly he was in a forest clearing at night. Stars were bright overhead and a full moon shone down on a group of men, chanting with arms raised to the skies, their backs marked by the same tattoo he had seen on his father. There was a sense of expectation in the air, a latent violence that compelled Blake to draw more closely to the group. He became aware of the stench of blood and stink of voided bowels, overlaid by the cool night air and forest scent.

Movement caught his eye from the trees behind the leader of the circle, a twitch in the shadow. Three bodies hung in the ash grove, and as he focused, Blake saw that their abdomens had been cut open. A rush of nausea gripped him; the men had been hanged with their own entrails and then wound again with rough ropes to hold their weight. One of the victims still jerked in place, his body refusing to give up the last spark of life.

"Great Odin, we call on you tonight. We relive the myth of Ymir and the creation of the world for your glory."

The leader's voice was rough yet powerful, rolling through the clearing so that every man could hear him clearly. Blake understood the words as his father had heard them all those years ago, for it was Magnus' terror he could feel, Magnus' eyes he saw through. He must have had the book with him at this occult ceremony performed on the edge of civilization years ago.

A man lay tied in the middle of the ring of followers, blood from his wounds dripping onto the grass. His eyes were closed but his chest rose and fell rapidly at the words intoned around him. The leader began a new chant, the words a repetitive phrase that rumbled from his chest. He stamped his feet slowly and the other men in the circle joined the incantation. The stamping grew faster and the repetition of the words spun through Blake's head like another voice taking over his brain. The thump of their feet resonated through the ground and his heart began to thud in time. The men drew hand axes from their belts as the chant reached a crescendo, and then they fell silent, staring at the victim in their midst.

Stepping forward, the leader grabbed the hair of the prone man.

"For you, Odin," he called to the sky, lifting his axe. Blake could almost feel the panicked state of the victim as he struggled and moaned. The leader brought down the weapon into the meaty part of the man's neck, pushing him to the floor as he hacked at the bony spine, blood spattering a dark wetness over his clothes. It took several blows to sever the head, then the leader lifted it to the sky with a primal roar as the men around him began to chant again.

Blake felt horror morph into shame, and then it struck him. His father had known the leader. This was his family; the leader was Magnus' own father. How many more sacrifices had he been involved in before he had fled this life for that of a preacher in London?

The leader gestured to two of the men, and they stepped forward with axes raised as the others continued to chant. Together the men began to butcher the body, blood soaking the earth. One of them smashed the skull so the brains ran out and made sure to separate the teeth from the jaw. It only took ten minutes to reduce a living man to body parts and gore. Blake retched, stomach heaving as he fell to his knees, unable to tear his gaze from the terrible sight. The eyes of the chanting men fell upon him as he coughed and spat, and then he saw the leader walking towards him with a determined stride, eyes wild with anger. Panicking, Blake pulled himself back out of the trance, dropping the book.

Retching and coughing, he found himself back in the bedroom, sweat dripping from his brow. He knelt on the floor, trying to anchor himself to this dimension, to this physical place. The visions had always been passive before, the very definition of remote viewing, but he had felt the eyes of the leader upon him and he had seen the intent to harm. Did that mean he could be physically hurt or even killed during a vision? Blake's mind reeled with the implications, even as the doubts about his own sanity flooded in, as they always did after a vision. Was it just some kind of hallucination, something he made up, even some kind of brain damage?

As he returned consciously to the bedroom, Blake could hear his mother praying in the room below, a singsong invocation to the God she had always trusted. In Magnus she had found a prophet, but even the great preacher must eventually stand before his God, and now it seemed, Precious had found her own voice. Blake couldn't fathom how she believed as she did, but hadn't he also seen things that proved there was more than a physical realm?

Still lightheaded, Blake reached for his smartphone and

googled Odin. During the attack of the Neo-Vikings on the British Museum a while back, he had learned a few things about the Norse god, but most of his knowledge came from Hollywood, rather than the original myths. Pages of articles came up, but one in particular caught his eye. The Norse peoples had believed that the universe originally emerged from an ancient being called Ymir. When Odin and the other deities had decided to create Earth, they murdered Ymir and made the world from his body, the sky from his skull and formed the clouds from his brains. His blood ran out to form the sea and his bones and teeth were seeds for the mountains. The men in the woods had been enacting this ancient myth in order to call on the power inherent in this primeval being. Odin was the god of frenzy and violent death, and bestowed wisdom and divine inspiration on his worshippers.

Reading on, Blake found that Odin had hung from an ash tree for nine days and nights to gain knowledge of the runes that could command great power. Human sacrifices to Odin were killed in a similar fashion to honor the god and also to represent Yggdrasil, the great ash tree that spanned the heavens, Earth and the underworld. This had been his father's past, some kind of cult that still worshipped the ancient gods in a modern world.

Blake flicked open the Galdrabók, trying to understand why Magnus had kept the book all these years. Why not burn it, or leave it behind when he started this new life? He turned the pages, noting drops of wax on some and marks like blood on others. The edge of one page was heavily marked with charcoal, a substance that lifted off onto Blake's fingertips. The page contained a series of runes and Icelandic spells for charisma, for the inner power to draw people in and make them follow. A wave of anger washed over Blake, and then a deep disappointment in the man he had both feared and worshipped.

He stood and walked downstairs, the book of runes in his hand. Precious knelt by the bed praying, and his father's eyes were locked on the space above the fireplace, where the demon had sat.

"I know what you were part of," Blake said, his voice strident, accusing. His father's eyes were flint hard.

CHAPTER 11

"I KNOW YOU TOOK part in human sacrifice rituals years ago."

Blake forced the words out. There was a moment of possibility when he could have been wrong but Magnus didn't blink, didn't even flinch.

"No!" Precious put a hand to her mouth, but Blake knew she could see he spoke the truth and there was no denial in his father's eyes. Weeping, she ran from the room and down the stairs. He heard the front door bang as she left to find solace in the forest. Part of him wanted to go after her, but this was a reckoning he couldn't run from anymore.

"What else did you do in exchange for the power of the runes?" Blake shouted. "Are these demons here to take what you traded for this new life?" He stepped close to the bed. "Do you think that I was given my visions as a curse because of what you did, or perhaps a gift that you should have had instead of me? Well, I want to see it. I want to see everything. I think you owe me that much."

Magnus closed his eyes for a moment, and Blake felt the stillness of the room, waiting for his answer. When his father opened his eyes again, Blake saw agreement, and a kind of relief that he could finally share this burden. He had been holding it alone for so long.

Blake held the Galdrabók close to the bed, and Magnus shifted a little so that his limp hand was thrust towards it. Blake laid it on the book, placing his own hand next to it as he slipped into the veils of consciousness, trying to surf the waves of his father's past. Images and sounds flooded his mind, taking him back in time as the shadows circled and he glimpsed an older world of deeper forests and high mountains. He delved further, seeking the sins that haunted Magnus now.

A scream ricocheted through his brain, splintering the vision. Blake's eyes flew open at the sound. The walls bled black and the spiked creatures crept closer to the bed. The floor writhed with a mass of bodies. One hissed at Blake, clambering up the chair next to him to reach the bed. Blake tried to push it off but his hands went right through it. He was still in trance but this wasn't the past – it was right now. Another scream and then a moan and he turned to see Magnus pinned down by several of the creatures. One was sucking the air from his lips and another had a hand inside his chest, squeezing his father's heart, seeping black pus into the man's blood.

"No," Blake shouted, trying in vain to pull the creatures off his father. But his hands could find no purchase in the other realm and the creatures paid him no heed, continuing to swarm. They began to rip strips of flesh from the old body, licking the wounds and dripping blood on the sheets. The thing on Magnus' back reared up and bared its fangs, pointed and dripping with venom. Blake could do nothing as it pierced the man's skull.

Waves of pain emanated from his father. Magnus shook, his breathing a rasp as he dragged air into his lungs, even as his chest was crushed by the number of creatures swarming over him. The demon at his head crunched its jaws down and Blake could see his father's skull begin to fragment. He babbled, desperately clutching at prayers his mother had taught him from a young age, snatching at scripture long forgotten. The demons were impervious, and as Magnus convulsed, they began to bite chunks from his skin.

Magnus screamed in Blake's head but no words came audibly from his throat. Blake wept, desperately pulling at the creatures but his fingers only found air. Magnus' skull split under the teeth of the demon and his brain could be seen pulsating, the veins bulbous on the creamy surface. As the demon peeled back the bone to feed, it met Blake's eyes and he saw the promise of Hell there. With a start, Blake pulled his hand from the Galdrabók, panting with terror. He could bear to see no more.

He was back in the lilac room, the only sound the rasp of Magnus' breath, coming slowly now, each one too many seconds apart. His body was barely shaking, and there was no evidence of that other dark reality. Blake wept, kneeling at his father's bedside, his mind flooded with the echo of the visions. Even with his eyes open, the room seemed to flicker from lilac to black as if his dual perception had melded into one reality.

Magnus took a last rattling breath, the gurgling from his throat a hideous wet noise, and then his chest was still.

"No," Blake whispered. "Not yet." He took his father's hand, feeling the warmth of his skin. The hand that had inflicted his own scars over years of abuse in the name of God. Blake kissed it, pressing his lips to Magnus' palm and in his mind, he pleaded for more time. Perhaps together they could revoke whatever hold the Galdrabók had over his father. But there was no further breath and Blake sensed an emptiness in the physical body in front of him. What had been his father was gone, and although the Elders and the congregation would believe that Magnus was in Heaven with his Lord, Blake could only see visions of his father consumed by the fiends of Hell.

The door banged downstairs and he heard his mother's

footsteps on the stair. Blake stood as she walked in. She saw the anguish in his eyes and pushed past him to the bed, pulling Magnus' body into her arms.

"No, no, no," she cried, tears coursing down her cheeks. "Oh my love, don't leave me."

Blake couldn't bear to watch his mother's suffering. He needed to get out of the house, for he sensed demonic eyes watching him, calling for him to return to that reality. Whatever the truth, he needed to forget, and there was only one sure way to drown these visions.

CHAPTER 12

As HER BIKE TOOK the final corner of the tree-lined road leading to the gates of Broadmoor Hospital, Jamie saw the main building looming ahead. It was an imposing structure, with red brick walls, arched windows and bands of lighter brown brick marking the floor levels inside. Bars on the windows betrayed the true nature of the place, for unlike most hospitals, people here were not free to leave. Jamie felt a sense of trepidation at going in, as if somehow this was all a trick and she would never emerge.

Broadmoor was one of the top-security mental hospitals in Britain, according to information Jamie had read that morning. It held several hundred male inmates, and had been designed by a military engineer in 1863 to house what were then known as criminal lunatics. It was originally intended for the reception, safe custody and treatment of people who had committed crimes while actually insane, or who had become insane while undergoing sentences of punishment. It had been a prison, but in 1948 Broadmoor became known as a hospital.

Jamie parked her bike and looked up at the building, its military bearing apparent in strong lines and heavy aspect. These days, its function was overlaid with medical jargon, but its residents were still the stuff of nightmares and tabloid frenzy. The Teacup Murderer, an expert poisoner; Peter Sutcliffe, the Yorkshire Ripper, and Kenneth Erskine, the Stockwell Strangler; the Krays, Ian Brady and even the inspiration for Hannibal Lecter, Robert Maudsley. In a particular gruesome incident in 1977 within these very walls, Maudsley and another prisoner had taken a pedophile into a cell, barricaded themselves inside and tortured him for nine hours, before garroting him and eating part of his brain with a spoon. Maudsley was now in solitary confinement in the basement of Wakefield Prison, in a two-cell glass cage, his furniture made of compressed cardboard. While most mental illness was considered by many to be an imbalance in brain chemistry, this level of psychopathy seemed to portray an entirely different brain altogether.

Jamie took off her bike clothes and added them to the panniers. She straightened her trousers and put on her jacket before walking to the gate. A man in a grey suit stood in the entrance hall, presumably the psychologist she was assigned to meet regarding the case. Although his suit looked a bit threadbare, the man's bearing was proudly aristocratic. Jamie had heard that Broadmoor was a highly sought location, a prestigious placement for any psychologist. It was so much more interesting than working with the general population whose troubles were mainly anxiety and depression, a banal litany of monotonous woe.

"Dr Taylor-Johnson?" Jamie asked, and the man nodded, holding out his hand in greeting.

"Welcome to our little piece of England, Detective. Let's get you through security and I'll show you around."

In the main entrance hall, Jamie put her things on a conveyor belt in the same fashion as airport security, and walked through the body-scan machine.

"If you wouldn't mind, Detective," Taylor-Johnson said. "We also need a photo for your ID card."

Jamie nodded, fascinated with the high level of security,

even for a short visit.

"Of course, it's not a prison," the psychologist said, noting her interest. "This is a hospital and we care for our patients." Jamie glanced out the window at the fifteen-foot mesh fence topped with overhang and razor-wire. There were cameras on every corner, facing both ways with one opposite so there were no blind spots. Taylor-Johnson followed her gaze and visibly bristled.

"Patients are detained and they're not free to leave, but that is for their own and other people's well-being. They can't be let out, but equally we can't let them loose in a prison." Jamie could hear a defensive tone in his voice. This was clearly a subject he had to address frequently. "Broadmoor provides physical, social and mental health care with the aim of rehabilitation."

"Is this reception area the main focus of your security?" Jamie asked.

"There's the physical security, of course," Taylor-Johnson said, "but we also have procedural security, counting the patients, and regular rounds, so we always know where everyone is. We have relational security, as well, and trust with the patients so they tell us when things are amiss. We also communicate with the control room, logging everyone's movements. It's a hospital," he emphasized again, "but these methods keep everybody safe."

"You have a control room?" Jamie asked, imagining banks of computers, no doubt similar to police monitoring stations. Humans were indeed the most dangerous predators, and this place looked ready to tackle any situation fast.

"Of course, but it's all for the patients' benefit, and to prevent any kind of … situation."

Jamie was aware that there had been a couple of escaped prisoners in Broadmoor's history. In 1952, serial killer John Straffen had murdered a young girl within hours of escaping, and since then, others had made it over that security wall. There was now a network of sirens that would sound in the nearby towns and villages in case of any escapees. Jamie thought briefly of the siege of Frankenstein's castle, the terror of suburbia at the approach of the monster. But these men looked ordinary, people you wouldn't even look at twice in the street, the monster only in the pathways of their own minds.

"Patients are constantly monitored," Taylor-Johnson continued as they walked through the hospital. "Of course, psychopharmacology is critical for treatment, and the drug dosage is adjusted based on an individual's behavior and response to medication. Patients also have three to nine months of assessment by a multi-disciplinary team while a care plan is developed."

"Do you have any problems with drug use inside?" Jamie asked, thinking of the store at the back of Monro's private office.

Taylor-Johnson shook his head, pausing at a reinforced glass panel.

"This is the drug bay and you can see it's all automated. Everything is highly controlled, and everyone is searched on the way in and out."

Jamie watched as a robot arm picked a packet of pills off a shelf and dispensed it to a slot where a nurse picked it up.

"Medication is critical for dampening the immediate symptoms and behavioral problems," Taylor-Johnson continued, seemingly intent on proving the safety of the hospital. "There's a broad range of choice in antipsychotics and anti-depressants these days, and we find the best combination for the patient with the minimum of side effects. Of course, the drugs may control some issues, but unfortunately they can't help with mending relationships or enabling the patient to return to real life, so we have other therapies for that."

As they continued to walk down the corridor, Jamie glanced into a side room. There were art projects laid out on benches, and a couple of men painting. Taylor-Johnson paused to explain.

"Illness doesn't get better without treatment and that takes time. Occupational therapy structures the day, so the patients have some kind of work to do, and we've found that patients engaging in meaningful activity don't act up."

Jamie could see that patients here had a reasonable quality of life. Broadmoor Hospital was now designed to care for and rehabilitate instead of functioning as a simple prison, but not all would agree that was appropriate.

"There are some people who think the men here are evil," she said. "And the things we see as police make many of us consider the world a dark place that might be better without these men in it." Jamie thought back to the drug-fueled murder she had witnessed in the caves beneath West Wycombe. "What do you think?"

Taylor-Johnson's eyes darkened, and she saw the conflict there as he considered his words carefully.

"Our aim is to care for and treat patients whose behavior could be a danger to others, in particular those with psychotic disorders. But typically these men have had traumatic childhoods and they've been punished severely in the past. They harm themselves and others as a way of managing the world. It's the only way they know. There are some here … well, let's just say that in the vast expanse of human behavior, there will always be extremes. These men exist on the very edge, so we call them insane and treat their madness. But our society can't say that they're evil, because we're rational, and rational people don't believe in evil. Do they, Detective?"

Jamie couldn't meet his gaze. To be honest, she didn't know anymore. Being in the police certainly ground down that rationality, and with what they saw every day, it was hard to believe that there wasn't some kind of chaotic force that drove some people to the depths, twisting them from loving fathers to abusive parents, from doting mothers to drug addicts who would leave their children for the next fix. If there was no evil force in the world, then that only left human nature to blame, and the potential to harm lay within everyone.

"Let's walk on, Detective." Taylor-Johnson continued down a side corridor, pointing out the various wings as they walked. Jamie found the place fascinating, a window into a life so far removed from normality. She noticed her mind was clearer than it had been in the last months of mourning, the intellectual stimulation of the case bringing her alive again.

"There are different types of wards," Taylor-Johnson explained. "This corridor has twelve side rooms – you could call them bedrooms – and each is the same. The furniture is built into the walls so there's nothing that could be used as a weapon or broken off to self-harm. Of course, the ward facilities are what the patients need, not what they want. It's not a hotel, and we expect patients to be up and engaging in some kind of activity every day, not lying in bed for hours. It depends on their illness, and at what point they are in their recovery, but we encourage patients to keep busy. Plus, there's a range of leisure activities, music and art, gardening, computers but no internet. We monitor everything they do and report back to the clinical team on their behavior. We've found that too much empty time makes people depressed."

That was certainly true, Jamie thought, and throwing herself back into work was certainly the best therapy for her own situation. She glanced inside one of the rooms, the plastic furniture rounded, as if designed for a child. She wondered what it must be like to be watched at all times, monitored in every activity, each twitch analyzed for signs of psychopathy and then medicated, forcefully if necessary, in order to modulate behavior. If she was watched twenty-four hours a day, would these doctors perceive the dark destruction that threatened her mind? Would they see that she craved the oblivion of final release?

Jamie realized her hands were tightly clenched and she relaxed them purposefully, exhaling slowly to calm herself again. This place made her feel claustrophobic, as if all these people could see inside her head and knew her darkest secrets. She had left a woman to die, savaged by a dog in bloodlust. She had brought death to those trapped in the Hellfire Caves. Jamie glanced over at Dr Taylor-Johnson, all buttoned up and superior. What secrets did he keep, and who saw into his head? Was the line between patient and keeper so thin as to be separated by action alone?

"Did you know Dr Christian Monro personally?" she asked, refocusing on the case.

The doctor's eyes flickered a little at her question.

"Yes, of course. As a forensic psychiatrist, he was a regular visitor and returned to reassess patients over time. We disagreed on some of his cases, but professional conflict is part of the game, Detective."

"Any case in particular?"

"Well, Timothy MacArnold, who you're interviewing today, would be one example of where we clashed. I'm still not sure the diagnosis was correct, but Monro was adamant that he be cared for here, and not sent to a high-security prison."

"What do you think is wrong with him?"

"We treat him for antisocial personality disorder and he has symptoms of schizophrenia, but some days, Detective … " The doctor shook his head. "I wonder whether these men are much cleverer than we assume."

"Doesn't research on psychopathy suggest that most people with the traits also display above-average intelligence?" Jamie asked.

"Yes, and with it, incredible powers of observation, as well as the ability to charm and flatter. We're all weak, Detective, and it's easier to believe that someone is telling the truth, but lies are surely the common currency in this place. Some days, I'm not so sure that psychopathy itself is a mental illness, and of course, many people on the psychopathic scale don't ever commit a crime. Perhaps it's more of a personality scale that we will only acknowledge when we're finally ready to embrace our own darker sides."

They stopped in front of an interview room.

"Timothy is in here, but he's known inside as Diamond Mac."

"Why's that?" Jamie asked.

"Oh, you'll see." Taylor-Johnson gave a wry smile. "He'll enjoy telling you himself. He's a clever man, and there are victims linked to him who still haven't been found. He won't admit to the murders, of course, only to the theft of diamonds that went missing at the same time the bodies were found."

The psychologist pushed open the door.

CHAPTER 13

INSIDE THE CELL-LIKE room, a man sat on the far side of a thick table. He wasn't physically restrained, but two stocky orderlies stood at either side of him, alert and watchful for any sudden movements.

Timothy MacArnold wore a t-shirt that matched his eyes, the grey of an English winter sky. His features were plain, an everyman no one would pick from a police line-up – or everyone would. His left arm was a wreck of scars, with broad stitches of white tissue. Jamie couldn't tell whether it was a tattoo or some form of self-mutilation.

"It's how I was able to steal as much as I did," MacArnold said, noting her gaze and grinning to reveal perfect white teeth. "I would cut into my skin, insert the diamonds and then sew myself together again. The gems became part of me, encrusted with my blood, my pus. They became part of my body ... until these bastards dug them out." He paused, meeting Jamie's eyes, and a prickle of sweat beaded in the small of her back at his cold stare. "I still feel their sharp edges when I wake alone in the dark. It keeps me focused on surviving so that one day I can feel that again. Now, Detective, please sit down."

He pointed to the chair in front of the desk, as if this was his office and he was their superior, summoning them to a meeting.

"And a good morning to you, Timothy." Dr Taylor-Johnson sat down at the table and beckoned Jamie to sit next to him. "Detective Brooke has a few questions for you about Doctor Monro."

"That bastard. He hasn't been in this week. Does that mean he's finally finished his thesis?"

"Thesis?" Jamie asked.

"He was writing about me. His pet psycho." MacArnold's tone was edged with pride. "Gonna get a book deal and everything."

"First I've heard of it," Taylor-Johnson said quickly, almost too fast. Jamie had the strange sensation that she couldn't tell who was lying anymore. This place had a force field that turned everything into double-speak and made her distrust her own gut, but there had been no manuscript at Monro's office. She pulled out her notebook.

"Dr Monro was murdered."

MacArnold laughed, throwing his head back so hard that the chair tipped slightly. The two orderlies grabbed at it, righting it gently. They had to protect the patient as well as the visitors. The laugh died quickly and Timothy's eyes were shining as he spoke.

"That's a bugger, but the bastard deserved it." He licked his lips. "How was he killed?"

"That information hasn't been made public yet," Jamie said. "No doubt it will be in the papers soon enough, but your name came up in the investigation."

MacArnold smiled. "You see the monitoring I'm subject to, Detective." He pointed up at his attentive guardians. "I am indeed a special man, but even I couldn't have escaped this prison for a night of what would have been a great pleasure, I'm sure."

"Do you know of anyone who might have wanted to harm Dr Monro? Anyone here?" Jamie asked.

"Monro got me in here, Detective, and for that I was

grateful. I'm 'rehabilitating,' and they tell me that one day …" He put his hands together as if in prayer. "I may emerge a changed man. For now, I embrace my own crazy line, for it makes me special enough to be amongst the chosen few in this place and not rotting in some stinking prison. I know Monro had his doubts about my sanity, or lack of it, but he said he could get me into a special government program next and my brain would make me a valuable asset." He paused, savoring the word. "Valuable, you see. So why would I want him dead? Without him, these bastards could reassess me as a violent criminal instead of mentally ill and I could be shunted off to the slammer. Couldn't you, Doc?"

On the streets, Jamie would have taken that tone as a threat. At this point, she would consider calling backup, but Taylor-Johnson shook his head gently, as if he heard this kind of talk all the time.

"We know you're ill, Timothy. Just give it time." He turned to Jamie. "That's the first I've heard of this special government program."

His tone suggested doubt that it even existed, but Jamie thought of the symbol on Monro's files and the man at the police station. Perhaps Timothy was telling the truth this time.

MacArnold cut in, his voice loud in order to focus their attention back on him.

"Monro wanted to know about my hobbies, Detective. I had just taken up taxidermy before I got caught. It's not easy to skin an animal, you know. You have to get its hide off like a coat and then duplicate the body in straw or other material and then stuff that skin again. Like a turkey, ready for roasting." He paused. "He used to ask me about sex, too."

Jamie didn't flinch, but she felt the others in the room tense, as if ready to stop him from speaking. She thought of Monro's hidden room, of the edges of pleasure and pain.

"What did he want to know?" she asked.

Timothy's eyes glinted. "You want to get off on it too, Detective. I bet you like a bad boy."

Dr Taylor-Johnson pushed back his chair. "Time to go, Detective. I'm sorry for this behavior."

Jamie stayed seated, addressing herself to Timothy.

"What did Monro want to know?"

Timothy smiled, baring the edges of his perfect white teeth. He touched the scars on his left arm gently, caressing the raised welts.

"He wanted to know if this was sexual. If I cut myself for pleasure."

Jamie held his eyes. "And do you?"

"Would that make me mad, Detective? Is that what you want? What if I cut you for pleasure, eh? What if I told you it makes me hard just thinking about your blood?"

Timothy's tone was almost impassive, with an edge of challenge. Jamie didn't flinch from Timothy's gaze and held it a moment longer. His power play was impotent here.

"I think that's all I need for now." She pushed back her chair.

"I did *not* say you could leave," Timothy banged his fists on the table, rising to his feet, leaning over the table, his face contorted with rage and hate. The two orderlies grabbed him and yanked him back as Taylor-Johnson pulled Jamie to her feet and the door opened to let them out.

One of the male nurses outside advanced with a syringe as the orderlies pushed Timothy face-down onto the table, holding him still as he was sedated. The sound of shouting soon dulled to a muted roar.

"I'm sorry," Taylor-Johnson said as he ushered Jamie down the corridor. "I don't think that was much use, and I apologize for Timothy's behavior."

Jamie shook her head. "I've seen and heard a lot worse, to be honest, and there aren't usually so many people around to help. I'm curious, though. Did you ever see any of Monro's research work?"

"I know a little of what he was looking into, but he was a radical in many people's eyes, embraced by those of an ultra-right-wing persuasion. He believed physical punishment was fitting for aspects of therapy, as a way to release some of the innate tension of conditions. He apparently met with Members of Parliament, those who would support the return of harsher sentences. He was also part of the campaign to reintroduce capital punishment."

"The death penalty?"

Taylor-Johnson nodded. "It's a surprisingly popular political request, especially in these difficult financial times. Taxpayers question how their hard-earned cash can fund a place like this, where men convicted of violent crime and multiple murder have their own rooms, are well fed and get to attend art classes. There are rumors that Monro's research would have provided some kind of platform for the right-wing political agenda against the rights of the mentally ill."

Jamie couldn't see how a civilized country like Britain would ever allow the death penalty when it condemned countries like China, Iran and Pakistan, while at the same time turning a blind eye to the United States. But she also knew of the right-wing leanings amongst certain groups including the police, many of whom supported a stronger deterrent to crime. After attending the aftermath of domestic violence and child abuse countless times, Jamie found herself struggling to defend the continued existence of those who did such things.

"What do you think about it?" she asked.

Taylor-Johnson sighed. "We all have to decide where the lines are, Detective. Between those who are mentally ill and can't help their actions versus those who voluntarily choose to give in to evil impulse. The rehabilitation of the mentally ill is my life's work, so I have to believe that those with true mental illness don't actively choose their path. We need to treat them with compassion, and hope that with therapy and continued medication, they can find their way back into society again. If Monro had his doubts, well, I can understand that. Sometimes, our belief and patience is stretched. But I've seen success here, and I'm sure you've seen evidence overturned against someone you believed guilty, Detective."

Jamie nodded, knowing that as much as she and her colleagues tried, the best was sometimes not good enough and rarely, but sometimes, they got it wrong.

"Thank you for your time, Doctor. I'll be in touch if there's anything else I need to know."

CHAPTER 14

BLAKE RAN ALONG THE track towards the main road, the Galdrabók heavy in his coat pocket. He needed to get away from the house, from the creatures that dragged his father's soul down to Hell, from his own memories of abuse. Part of him knew he should stay and comfort his mother, be the son she needed, but he couldn't face her perfect memory of the man he now knew as tainted. The images of dark creatures gnawing at his father's body kept looping round his mind and the edge of desperation was making him crazy. The need to drink was overwhelming, and Blake clenched his fists to hold back the anxiety the craving brought with it.

He walked towards the nearest town, keeping his thumb out as cars passed. Rain began to drizzle down and soon a car stopped.

"You alright, son?" The man was older than Magnus had been, his eyes a welcoming warm brown. "Not a great night to be hitching. Where you going?"

"Train station, if that's OK."

It wasn't far and the man seemed happy to chat with nothing more than a few grunts from Blake in return. At the station, Blake waved the man goodbye and looked at the ticket office, the entrance almost obscured by the now-pouring rain. In Britain, the nearest pub was never too far away and Blake caught sight of one just behind the car park, lights in the window promising beer and warmth. He needed the oblivion that only alcohol could bring right now, even in this shitty little corner of England. Maybe especially here.

The Bear and Staff was teetering on the edge of rundown, with old stools and wooden tables flawed by ring marks, overlaying each other through years of use. There were a couple of people drinking inside, a group of men who looked like they kept the place going with their custom, and several clearly waiting for the train. The bartender looked up with expectation as Blake walked in, smiling as he approached the counter.

"Two tequilas please, and …" Blake looked at the wide selection of ales on tap. "Two pints of Abbeydale's Black Mass."

The British penchant for exotically named ales seemed strangely appropriate given his visions, but already Blake doubted what he had seen. There was no way he could verify the facts of the Scandinavian murders quickly, and the black creatures could have been a result of the pain-relief drugs Magnus had been on. Somehow Blake's visions must have tapped into that perception, because of course, there was no such thing as demons.

The barman nodded. "Coming right up. You waiting for someone?"

He put the tequila shots on the bar, glancing down at Blake's gloved hands.

"Something like that." Blake downed the shots one after the other. The burning in his throat anchored him to this place, in this time, a physical sensation that he had never felt in any vision and helped him center with reality. The immediate rush took the edge off his craving, but oblivion had become harder to reach of late. The barman placed the beers on the bar.

"Two more tequilas," Blake said, handing over extra cash.

"Must be one hell of a bad day," the barman said, turning to pour more shots. He put a bag of salted crisps next to them. "You'd better have these, too."

The door banged and a whistle of wind rushed in, bringing a taste of rain into the dank bar. Blake glanced up as he gulped at the first beer. Two men in dark coats walked to the far end of the bar, collars turned up against the weather. One of the men looked over, piercing grey eyes raking over Blake's taut face. Could they see the twisted mass inside him, or was that just paranoia? What did it even matter? Blake thought, downing the beer in just a few gulps. He didn't care what anyone thought of him here. He only needed to blur the edges of the world as fast as possible.

His phone rang. Checking the number, he saw it was his mother. He let it go to voicemail, guilt washing over him. But he couldn't face her grief, or her unquestioning faith that Magnus would be waiting for her in Heaven.

Blake downed the next two tequilas, savoring the raw power of the spirit. Distilled from the agave plant, it survived harsh desert winds, its spiked leaves warding off predators. Blake drew on that strength now, letting the alcohol work its magic. His limbs began to feel heavy and, finally, his breathing slowed to a more even rhythm and anxiety abated.

He pulled the Galdrabók from his pocket, running gloved fingertips across the surface of burnished leather. Whatever past it represented, that was gone now, and this was all he had left to remember his father by. This and the scars. Could his gift really be a punishment from the gods in recompense for his father's sin? Or was there something wrong in his brain? That thought always teetered on the edge of his consciousness and some days he would give anything to have this curse removed. Blake took another sip of the beer … if he kept on drinking this way, he would likely get his wish.

There was one person who made him want to stop drinking for good, and Blake found a shadow of a smile on his lips at the thought of Jamie Brooke. The desire to speak to her welled up inside. Her perspective on Magnus and the visions might make everything clearer. She would know he was on the edge of drunk, but Jamie had seen him in a worse state when she had come to him desperate for help in the middle of the night.

Blake stood, placing his hand on the table to steady himself as his head spun, the pub fading in and out of focus. The group of regulars looked at him, their stares hostile, hands wrapped tightly around their pint glasses. Blake nodded at them as he walked towards the door, pulling it open with one hand as he fumbled for Jamie's number on his phone.

Outside, the air was crisp and chill. The heavy rain had morphed into that peculiarly British drizzle that barely seemed there but still soaked anyone standing in it. The tarmac was shining purple with oil marks from the car park, light from the street lamps turning the dark pools into rainbows. Blake turned towards the back of the pub and headed for a doorway with some shelter. As he heard the first rings on Jamie's phone, the door opened behind him. The two men from the bar came out, looked around and spotted Blake in the doorway. The man with grey eyes smiled, taking out a cigarette and lighting it as the other man walked wide, blocking Blake's exit to the car park.

The drunken haze couldn't hide the implied threat and Blake's heart thumped hard against his chest as the men advanced. He felt a trickle of sweat inch down his spine and cursed the amount of tequila he had drunk. His awareness was dulled, his mind heavy, his limbs sluggish. Jamie's line went to voicemail and Blake hung up, focusing on the men in front of him.

"Can I help you with anything?" he asked. "I'm just waiting for a friend."

The grey-eyed man took a long drag on his cigarette.

"I don't think anyone's coming for you." He indicated the other man. "Except us, of course. And we're friends, really, we are. You just have to get in the car with us."

Blake looked around him, checking for anything he could use as a weapon. "I think you must have the wrong person. I don't know you."

"Oh, but we know you, Blake Daniel." The grey-eyed man took another drag and dropped his cigarette to the wet ground, grinding it into a puddle. Blake's eyes flitted to the other man, who moved like a boxer – light on his feet but with surely a hell of a punch. Blake wasn't much of a fighter, but the beatings his father and the Elders dealt in his childhood had cured any fear of physical hurt.

"What do you want?" he asked.

The grey-eyed man pulled a box from a pocket inside his jacket.

"You have a remarkable gift, and we want to help you understand it. But if you're not going to come willingly, then it's our – qualified – medical opinion that your mental health issues are putting yourself and others at risk." The other man advanced, arms stretched wide, his eyes inviting Blake to move, to resist. He clearly relished the chance to inflict pain and Blake's heart rate spiked as he saw the grey-eyed man pull a syringe from the case. "For those who may inquire, we had to sedate you in order to prevent further injury to yourself and others in the vicinity. You had to be detained under the Mental Health Act, and, of course, you will have the right to appeal."

Move! Blake's mind screamed at him, but his body was leaden, his responses dulled. He just needed to get to the car park, where someone might see him and help, or at least he might be picked up on security cameras. The men took one more step towards him. Blake ducked low and charged the gap between them.

The thump of an elbow in his back knocked him to the

ground. A boot slammed into his side and Blake curled on one side, arms thrown up to protect his head as the blows thudded into his body. His phone went skidding beneath a skip in the alleyway.

"Enough." The grey-eyed man called a halt to the beating. Blake coughed and retched, gasping for air as he fought the spasms in his stomach. The stocky man grabbed his arm and flipped him over onto his back. For a brief moment, Blake felt the rain on his face as a blessing, melting away the reality of where he lay. Grey eyes came into focus in front of his face, and the man grinned as he pushed the syringe into Blake's neck. As his breathing slowed, Blake felt resignation settle within him, like a warm stone anchoring him to the earth. What could they do to him that he hadn't already faced in his visions? He shut his eyes and let the rain soak through him into the hard ground beneath.

CHAPTER 15

JAMIE PUT DOWN THE phone. She'd just missed Blake's call and he hadn't answered when she called back. Her finger hovered over redial, and then she shook her head, smiling a little. He was probably out somewhere in a noisy bar and couldn't hear the ring. With a stab of loneliness, she turned to the bookshelf where the terracotta urn sat in pride of place. She gently cupped it with her hand, the coolness on her palm reminding her that this was just a dead object. It might contain the physical remains of her daughter, but in itself, it was nothing. So why couldn't she just scatter the ashes in the bluebell woods that Polly had loved so much? Or throw them to the wind over the ocean? Why keep them here, grey dust and ashes that in no way represented the girl she had lost.

Jamie bent her forehead to the urn and knew she was still tethered to the memories. If she scattered these final grains of what had once been life, then she was utterly alone in the world. She thought of the bottle of sleeping pills in the bathroom, the oblivion that would take her away from this constant ache in her chest. Jamie breathed out, a long exhalation. The only way to deal with grief was to work. She walked to the kitchen and poured herself a large glass of pinot noir, taking it back to the sofa. Pulling out her cigarettes, she lit one and the long drag coupled with the wine gave her the tiny boost she needed. She opened Lyssa's diary and began to read.

They say it's chemistry in my brain that makes me this way. That some invisible chain of neurons has become polluted. The blackness sits in my head like a cancerous growth. In the past, they could have dug it out of my skull, lobotomized me and turned me into a loon, destroying the bad along with the rest of me.

Now, they pass electricity through my brain and try to buzz it out. With anesthetic, of course, as if that negates the barbarity. I imagine it fracturing into pieces, tiny shards of its disease spreading through the rest of my body. They say ECT is like a reset button, that I'm just a computer that needs a control-alt-delete reboot. They know best. Don't they?

But what if this blackness is just a part of me, not separate. What if it is bound into every atom of my body, making up who I am? When they try to rip it from me, or sedate it, or electroshock it away, the rest of me curls into a desperate ball, because they're destroying all of me. I am every color on the spectrum and black is necessary to highlight the bright yellow, and iridescent green, to enable brilliant turquoise to shine. Without black, there is no contrast, and without contrast, life is monochrome.

Jamie laid the diary aside. It was strange, but the overwhelming sense in Lyssa's words was life, a vibrant passion for living and creativity and an intelligent consideration of what life really was. The woman had been a dynamo, whirling through existence, and then she had crashed, ending it all. Jamie looked up at the terracotta urn. Polly had told her to dance, to continue to live, so tonight she would dance in remembrance of her daughter, and for Lyssa. Crushing the end of her cigarette into the ashtray, Jamie packed a bag quickly with her tango clothes and went out into the night.

***

Within thirty minutes, Jamie was at the *milonga*. She changed into her silver dress, the one Polly had loved her to wear. She slipped on tall heels, feeling her leg muscles elongate, the accentuation of her form. She pulled the clasp from her hair, letting the black cascade brush at her nape, as ghostly fingers of sensation ran down her spine. It was time to embrace this side of herself again, and in the dance, she could forget the complexities of the case.

The dim light in the room caressed the bodies of those who moved to the *tanda*, the grace of couples who clasped each other, some for one dance only and others for a lifetime. Jamie found divinity in the movement of human form as the *bandoneón* told of heartbreak and loss, the end of what was once perfect, but only for a heartbeat. Tango sublimated the dark soul through a repetitive beat, a singing in the blood that compelled the body to dance as if it no longer belonged to the brain. The noise in Jamie's head only subsided here, in the arms of a partner who cared only how their bodies moved together in the moment.

She caught Sebastian's eye across the room, her sometime dancing partner sensing her need. Between songs, he came to her and she stepped into his close embrace, no words necessary between them, only the challenge and acceptance of eye contact. There should be smoke here, Jamie thought, its haze casting a pall on the crowd who danced together as if the end of the world would come with the sun tomorrow. Tonight, the dancers would live as if for the final time, like the story of the rose and the nightingale, whose song was sweetest as the thorn pierced its dying breast.

Limbs were heavy until the music picked up, and the dance an automatic response to the call of the *milonga*. A primal beat, a need that must be fulfilled, an unbidden compulsion. The sound of the violin filled the room, strains of music that turned the mind from earthly pain into heavenly suffering. Surely the angels dance tango alongside pitiful humanity, and in doing so, transform their grief to something holy.

In the thrill of the dance, Jamie wrapped her leg around Sebastian's muscular one, her *ocho* a perfection of touch and release, a sensual play on the level of desire. She felt the twitch of something deep within her, a need to be touched, a need to be taken. A glimmer of it had surfaced when she had seen Blake this morning and now she recognized its significance. It was a flicker of life, when the body became music, a vessel for something beautiful that drove out the darkness within.

Tango chose me. The words came to Jamie unbidden. Tango threw its lovers together, letting them burn the flame for a pinch in time and then allowing them to slip away, burned and spent. The time in the dance was the only thing that mattered, and Jamie was already burned. Her thoughts returned to the morgue, deep underground, populated by dead babies, the remains of grotesque experimentation. That night in the Hellfire Caves, she had burned a part of herself away as Polly's body went to the god of flame in the caves. She still woke in the night with the taste of smoke in her mouth, but here she could let it all go. The color of tango was holy saffron that draped the pyres of the dead, of brilliant flame that burned the body until it was gone and darkest midnight blue, of the sky after the soul has returned to the stars.

Jamie felt Sebastian's arm around her waist and her body slid onto his, slid around it, flowing as she let herself go into the music, her *ocho* perfection. The tango connection was fleeting, the full length of the body during the dance and then the release. When the connection was broken, both must walk away, for what is perfect within the dance could only be something less if taken any further. Jamie held to this truth as the music came to an end. She walked away without looking back as Sebastian moved on to his next partner, a part of her left in the echo of his embrace.

CHAPTER 16

THE CANON CHANCELLOR, REVEREND Dr Martin Gillingham, began the slow walk around the cathedral, his ritual before leaving late each night. In the bustle of the busy daily life of St Paul's, it was too easy to forget why they all labored here. *This is the house of God, and here shall He be glorified*, Martin thought, looking up into the vast vaulted ceiling above him.

Of course, there were days when his faith wavered, as for any man, but today Martin felt a welling of the spirit, a divine refreshment that washed over him. He surveyed the holy domain, checking the corners behind the monuments, making sure the cathedral would be ready for another day.

"Thank you, Lord," he whispered, a smile on his face at how fortunate he was to work here, at the heart of Christian faith in London. He always walked this final round after most had gone home, and in the peace and quiet he could reconcile his mission with the fact that no one waited for him at his meager flat. His whole life was here, and perhaps his shade would walk this round after death, an imprint of faithful devotion. To die as a martyr for God was indeed a glorious way to enter Heaven triumphant, but Martin was content with a quiet life of service and solitude.

He passed one of the cathedral's most beloved paintings,

William Holman Hunt's *The Light of the World*. A cloaked Jesus stood in a verdant wood at night, surrounded by an abundance of branches, leaves and fruit. His face was peaceful and his eyes stared out of the canvas, inviting the watcher into his world. In his left hand, Jesus held a lantern which cast the warmth of candlelight onto his face and clothes, highlighting the ruddy colors. In a cathedral that valued all faiths, the lantern reflected its diversity with cutouts in the shape of the Star of David for Judaism and a crescent moon for Islam. Martin loved the painting, seeing in it the invitation of Jesus to join him on the Christian journey for another day.

He walked down the stone stairs to the crypt, looking up at the three death's-head skulls that marked the entrance. *For dust you are, and to dust you will return*, he thought and sighed. *Every day takes us closer to the grave and every day we must live for the glory of God.* At the bottom of the stairs, Martin turned right towards the tomb of Lord Horatio Nelson, walking across the intricate mosaic of anchors, sea monsters and scalloped patterns. A huge black marble tomb dominated the chamber, topped by Nelson's Viscount coronet. The sarcophagus had originally been made for Cardinal Wolsey, Lord Chancellor during the reign of Henry VIII, but when he had fallen from favor, it had been kept for someone more worthy. Nelson was surely deserving of such high honor, Martin thought, running his finger gently along the dark stone, yet the military man would likely have scorned the marble as too grand for a soldier. Martin was glad that underneath the monument, Nelson's earthly remains lay in a coffin made from the timber of one of the French ships he had defeated in battle.

Some thought that the obsession with honoring war was too dominant at St Paul's, but Martin understood that England could not stand without the courage of those who gave their lives in combat. This church would be nothing without military might, and Nelson's naval prowess was just one facet of glorifying God. After all, the Bible was filled with divine vengeance against those who would oppress, and this was a fitting memorial to one who brought victory for the glory of God and country.

A sharp clang sounded through the crypt, and Martin started, his hand grasping the smooth marble of the tomb. He stood still for a moment, listening, but there was no further noise. Perhaps it was one of the cleaners or security staff? The cathedral was never truly empty, but he knew the customary route of the support team and usually avoided them, moving into the spaces they vacated. After years of routine, the noise was unusual, and Martin felt a bristling under his skin, a rightful devotion for his church. Nothing must be out of place in the Lord's house.

He walked through the arches towards the Chapel of St Faith. It had once been a parish church attached to the old cathedral, and was now the official Chapel of the Order of the British Empire, where those awarded an OBE could be married or baptized. Martin's footsteps were soft on the gigantic flagstones, engraved in memory of those who had fought and died for Great Britain, the sleeping dead. The lamps were still glowing, surrounded by flames etched in metal, and the light caught the memorial of Florence Nightingale as he passed. Some had protested the inclusion of women in this chapel of war memory, but Martin found the nurse's calm face a blessing as she leaned over a dying man to give him water.

The noise came again.

Now that he was closer, Martin could tell that it came from the side chapel where the Holy Sacrament was kept. It was a sacred place, locked up tight, as no one was allowed there after the Host had been blessed in readiness for the service. Martin's heart beat faster. There was definitely something wrong here. This was not routine; this was not as it should be. He crept forward slowly. It was probably nothing, surely a mistake, but he had to be sure.

The wooden door to the side chapel was open a crack, and Martin peered through the space. He saw a man bent over the Communion wine, a hooded top obscuring his face. He seemed to be injecting something into one of the bottles. Martin frowned and pushed open the door, his righteous anger and concern overcoming any fear.

"What are you doing?" he said, stepping into the chapel. "This is a sacred place. Get away from those bottles."

The man slowly put down the syringe and held his hands up as he turned around, his face still in shadow. He said nothing, just stared, his head on one side as if considering the situation.

"It's OK," Martin said, taking another step towards the man, thinking of the security team. Their rounds down here weren't for another twenty minutes. "Let's go upstairs and I'm sure we can sort all this out." He held out open palms, a gesture of acceptance and welcome he had perfected after years of greeting parishioners.

The man moved suddenly, grabbing one of the Communion wine bottles by the neck and using it as a club. Before Martin truly saw it, the blow exploded on his jawbone. He reeled back, clutching his face, momentarily stunned. He hadn't been hit since he was a boy. Through the pain was a strange kind of relief that his physical body could still feel. But then the man raised the bottle again.

Martin stumbled backwards into the crypt, calling for help even as he knew that the thick walls would shield his cries from those above. The man came after him, arm raised, the bottle glinting in the light.

"I'm sorry," he whispered, "but this must be done. You shouldn't have come down here, but now you will serve as another example."

Martin couldn't keep his eyes from the weapon. In his

haste to escape, he tripped over one of the flagstones, falling to the floor. The harsh stone stung his hands, as the words of the dead rubbed at his flesh.

"Please," he begged, his voice slurred. "I can get you whatever you need. It doesn't have to be this way."

The man stepped over to him and Martin raised his arms to shield his head. Another blunt blow smashed into his forearm and he moaned, an animal sound that barely registered as human. Scrambling now, he dragged himself towards the altar under the watchful eyes of the famous artists and scientists carved into the wall of memorial plaques.

Martin felt another blow to the back of his head and the world exploded, pain mingling with warmth and then a tingling sensation in his limbs as he fell forward. *Oh, my Lord*, Martin prayed in desperation, *let me live. I'm not ready to die. Take this cup from me.* He felt a sob rise in his chest as he gasped for breath, forcing himself to turn over and face his tormentor. The man was pulling something out of his backpack now, a silver spike and a hammer. Martin's stomach wrenched at the thought of what he might do with it. He reached his arms out to the memorials around him, Turner, Millais and William Blake, luminaries of British culture. Their stone eyes looked down upon his suffering as the man advanced. As Martin's vision began to blur, he thought he heard weeping and the rush of angel wings.

CHAPTER 17

THE SUN WAS BARELY up and Jamie gulped at her large black coffee, trying to shake off the heaviness from lack of sleep after her night at tango. Blake hadn't called back and her texts had gone unanswered, so this morning she had used the police databases to get through to his mother at the family home. The distraught woman had told her of the death of Blake's father, and Jamie had vivid thoughts of Blake drinking in some dive bar, escaping into oblivion to forget his pain. She had seen him in that state before, and remembered how she had almost crept into bed with him one night. After months of relying on his upbeat support, she was torn by guilt that she hadn't been there for him in his grief. She would have to trust that he would come to her when he was ready.

As rays of early morning sun shone on the golden dome of St Paul's, Jamie felt a rush of patriotism, a moment of pleasure and pride at working in the greatest city on Earth. There had been a place of Christian worship at this site since 604 AD, but the iconic dome had been built by Sir Christopher Wren after the Great Fire of London had gutted the church in the seventeenth century. The pride of the capital during the Blitz, the dome had not been bombed, but emerged from the smoke, still standing even as the rest of the city burned. Looking up at the magnificent cupola, Jamie wondered whether it pleased God or man more. Certainly the towering grandeur directed all eyes to the sky, but what then? Jamie felt cool rain spotting her upturned face. Then there was only emptiness, a vaulted Heaven with a God who let children die in pain. Jamie shook her head – it was time to focus on work.

Missinghall spoke with the officer on the door and they entered the cathedral, footsteps echoing in the enormous space, usually filled with tourists but now empty as the crime scene was processed in the crypt. The nave was paved with black and white marble, a chessboard representing the struggle of good and evil. Jamie remembered seeing the same motif draped over Hindu gods in Bali, back before her 'real' life had started, before Polly and the police.

She glanced to her left as they walked down the center of the nave. Two angels guarded a door, one with a sword, the other a trumpet, their wings elegantly draping the floor, faces in repose. Above the door, a scrolled parchment pronounced, *Through the gate of death we pass to our joyful resurrection*. Jamie had a momentary sense that the door was a portal: that on the other side was another world, where Polly danced. She shook her head, the brief illusion shattered. She definitely needed more sleep.

The somber atmosphere invited reflection, and they walked in silence, looking up at the intricate decoration that dominated this end of the cathedral. The ceiling of the quire was rich with mosaics of creation, so detailed that the abundance flowed into the rest of the church. Three inset roundels depicted palm trees and all kinds of land animals, an azure ocean with spouting whales and flying fish, fruit trees and birds against a golden haloed sun. In the south quire, Jamie looked up at the face of John Donne, a shrouded effigy in marble. A former Dean of St Paul's, his writing praised the God he worshipped and his poetry was still studied in British schools. *No man is an island, entire of itself*, Jamie thought, the words echoing in her mind from lessons many years ago.

The cathedral was filled with tributes to the military might of Empire, with larger-than-life-size statues of men of war commemorated for their battle triumph. It seemed incongruous in a house of God to have such symbols of death, men who had slaughtered the ancestors of those who were now British themselves. Behind the altar was even a book of the American dead in the Second World War, its pages turned every day by the priests in commemoration of lives given in service.

Classical statues of the great men of the early church looked down upon the Whispering Gallery, and in the dome, sepia paintings portrayed the life of St Paul, transformed on the road to Damascus from persecutor to believer. Between the arches of the cupola were mosaics depicting the Old Testament prophets, Isaiah, Jeremiah, Ezekiel and Daniel as well as the four evangelists, Matthew, Mark, Luke and John. All the luminaries of the Bible were here, gazing down at believers as they worshipped, witnessing how much the simple carpenter's faith had changed the world.

Jamie and Missinghall walked down the stairs towards the muted murmur of the crime scene contained within the lower levels. After suiting up and signing the log, they entered the crypt. It was lit by small candelabra, their light shaded by metal flames, casting a warm glow into the stone space. The ceiling was low and the floor uneven with huge flagstones, which on closer inspection, Jamie realized were all tombstones of the honored dead. The usual bustle of the SOCOs was muted by thick walls and their respect for the house of worship.

The body lay at the base of a wall on the right side of a modern altar, designed to honor those who held the OBE, and flanked by their standards. Blood stained the plaque above the corpse, and Jamie noticed it was a tribute to William Blake, artist, poet and mystic, considered mad in his lifetime. It was carved with a quote from one of his most famous poems, *To see a world in a grain of sand And a heaven in a wild flower, Hold infinity in the palm of your hand, And eternity in an hour.*

"This is a strange one," forensic pathologist Mike Skinner said as he stood and walked towards them, careful to step around the perimeter. "There's evidence of blunt-force trauma to the head and body, but then the man's eyeball was pierced by that." He pointed to a long spike with a flared end on the flagstone near the body. The sharp end was coated in blood, clearly visible as the flash of the crime-scene photographer lit up the silver surface. "There's also a medical hammer lying on the other side of the body, used to bang the spike into the man's brain."

"Would that have killed him?" Missinghall asked, his face displaying distaste at the description.

Skinner shook his head. "No, I think he may have even been dead when the pick was inserted so it's more symbolic. I'll have to check it during the autopsy, but I've seen these instruments before in medical history magazines. The spike is a lobotomy orbitoclast icepick used for severing the connections in the prefrontal cortex after insertion through the corner of the eyeball. The mallet was used to drive the pick through the thin layer of bone and into the brain, where it was rotated back and forth." Missinghall looked disturbed as Skinner continued. "Very popular in the United States in the 1930s and '40s of course, but we did enough lobotomies here, too. Brutal, nasty stuff." Skinner shook his head. "Didn't kill most patients, but turned them into vegetables."

"It's got to be related to the murder of Christian Monro," Jamie said. "The link to madness is too much of a coincidence." She left out the matter of Blake Daniel predicting more murders. "Al, do we know if there's any evidence of theft?"

Missinghall shook his head as he checked the notes sent from first responders. "No, the Dean has said that nothing is missing, but perhaps the Canon disturbed someone?"

Jamie looked around the crypt. "But who and why? What could possibly happen down here that would warrant murder?"

Missinghall shrugged. "Sex, maybe drugs. Something that a churchman might disapprove of."

"We need to know more about the Canon Chancellor," Jamie said. "What was he involved in that could have led to his death?"

"We'll be out of here soon enough," Skinner said. "We can secure this area for the crime scene, but we've been told that nothing stops the Sunday service, so we have to get the bulk of processing done ASAP and get out of here." He looked at his watch. "Only a few hours to go, so I'd best get back to it."

CHAPTER 18

Shadows shifted in his mind and Blake became aware of his breath, the rise and fall of his chest, and the sound of medical monitors. His head thumped with the familiar rhythm of a hangover, but it wasn't as bad as it should be. He could smell antiseptic, and his skin prickled with goosebumps from cool air conditioning.

Blake opened his eyes. The light was dim but he was clearly in some kind of hospital room. A curtain surrounded his bed, patterned with swirls that made his stomach heave to look at. He closed his eyes again, concentrating on breathing evenly as his body calmed. His ribs ached and his torso was bruised. He remembered the car park, the beating, the two men. He lifted his hand to feel where the pain centered, but it was brought up short by a rattle on the metal bars at the side of the bed. He looked down and could just make out the padded handcuffs that shackled him.

There was a drip attached to a cannula in the back of his right hand. His gloves were gone, leaving his scarred hands vulnerable to the air and, in the dim light, the ivory ropes of damaged skin seemed to glow. His fingertips felt every puff of air in the room, and it seemed that the hangover was making him excruciatingly sensitive. Blake looked around for his clothes and the Galdrabók, the only thing he had left of his father. The fact of Magnus' death resounded through Blake, the absence a finality he had been waiting for all these years. But after what he had seen in that room, he was left with more questions than closure.

Blake shook his hands, tugging on the handcuffs until his heart thumped with the exertion and pain in his head spiked, bringing a wave of nausea. Doubt swirled through his mind. Perhaps he deserved to be here; perhaps he really was mentally ill. Were the hallucinations he had seen with his father evidence that he had gone over the edge?

A sound came from beyond the curtain, a footstep on the tiled floor.

"Is anyone there?" Blake called, his voice a croak. He swallowed, trying again, pushing himself up. "Please, can you tell me where I am?"

The footsteps faltered and then continued. Blake fell back onto the pillows, tension easing in his torso as he relaxed the injured muscles.

A moment later, the light came on and other footsteps approached, sure-footed, confident. The curtain swung back and a man in a white coat stood there. In the room behind him, Blake caught a glimpse of a dentist-style chair, with heavy restraints at the wrists, ankles, waist and neck. Above it was a head brace that could be lowered down so the skull could be held still during stereotactic brain surgery. Machines with wires and electrodes and trays of medical instruments stood on wheeled trolleys near the chair. Blake couldn't help but consider why he was in this particular room. He swallowed, easing his dry throat.

"Good to see you're back with us, Blake."

The man was completely bald with a strangely shaped head, and his eyes were different colors, one blue and one brown. His smile showed perfect white teeth. His angular jaw and prominent cheekbones demonstrated a disciplined diet and he must have been over fifty, although he had the smooth skin of Botox around his eyes and forehead.

"Recovered from your night out?"

The man's voice was mocking and Blake's mind flashed back to the alleyway by the pub. He wanted to smash the metal handcuffs into the man's face, but he could only clench his fists.

"Where am I?" he asked, his voice even and calm, not wanting to give the man any pleasure in his reaction.

The doctor walked around the bed to check on the drip, adjusting the flow rate.

"You're at a private hospital for people with mental illness. I'm Dr Damian Crowther, and you're under my care. As well as providing the very best treatment for our guests here, we perform research on the outer limits of perception."

Blake felt a flicker of his own self-doubt. "I've never even seen a psychiatrist, so why am I here?"

"We've heard reports of your visions, and how they've been helpful in solving certain crimes." The doctor bent and stroked a finger along the scars on the back of Blake's hand. "You have a gift we're interested in researching ..." He stood and his voice changed, an edge of hardness creeping in. "Your visions may just be an aberration we can cut out of your brain but just imagine the potential if it can be replicated." Crowther's eyes blazed with fanaticism. "The human mind is the last frontier. Those who come here add to the meager knowledge we have so far on the potential of humanity. Our remit is to pursue high-risk research in order to gain an intelligence advantage, and those who make it through the procedures have given their country a valuable service."

Blake's mind raced at the possibilities of experimentation. He looked beyond the curtains at the restraints on the chair.

"And those who don't make it through your ... procedures?" Blake asked, remembering Jamie mentioning a girl who had committed suicide after Monro's psychiatric treatment.

Crowther shrugged.

"The mentally ill are perceived as unstable, at risk. Their families are often relieved to have them controlled by medication and are pleased to have them incarcerated here, whether voluntary or committed. We've even had subjects delivered to our doors, the families begging for help. So, what is the real loss if the subjects pass on during testing?" He smiled, and Blake saw a glimmer of delight in his eyes. "For many of those, suicide becomes a life choice, and if we help them with that after we've learned all we can … Well, we're just saving taxpayers money. But you're a different matter altogether."

Crowther walked over to the bench on the far side of the room and picked up the Galdrabók. "This book is full of things I want to talk to you about." He opened the pages and pulled out the handwritten family tree. "But this evidence of your genealogical history is the real gold. Do you know what the rune next to your name means?"

Blake waited a second and then shook his head, overwhelmed by his desire to know more.

"The symbol is a mixture of the runes for madness, but also for power and supernatural insight. The ancient Greeks used the same word for madness and genius, and the Nordic culture believed the same thing. The runes imply that your father possessed the same gifts as you."

Blake closed his eyes, reliving the horror of his father's last moments as the dark creatures bit into his flesh. Magnus had tried to beat the gift from his son, because he suffered from its enhanced perception himself. Tears welled up as Blake wished for the years back. Together they could have worked out what it was, together they might have found an answer. He pushed the emotion down as Crowther continued.

"It would have been truly marvelous to have you both here. I could have compared the generational effect and even split out the genetics of your line to isolate the key to what gives you this remarkable gift." There was jealousy in his voice, Blake noted. An edge of desire for that which he didn't possess. Crowther opened a drawer and pulled out a syringe and a tourniquet. "For now, we'll have to start with DNA testing and genetic markers for the more common mental health issues." Blake struggled as Crowther walked to the bed. "If you struggle, it will hurt more. It's just a little needle stick, after all. And I know you're curious about your past."

With one last tug on his handcuffs, Blake realized he couldn't stop Crowther and he stilled, allowing the doctor to wrap the tourniquet round and draw the blood. The crimson liquid filled several glass vials. Blake couldn't help but wonder whether there was something different about his physiology, and his mind reeled with the implications of his family's genetic history. There were runes marked on other branches of the tree. There were more like him, cousins perhaps, people who could see just as he did.

Crowther finished with the extraction and removed the tourniquet. A drop of blood dripped from the tiny wound and ran down Blake's arm. The ache made him want to rub it, but the cuffs were still tight around his wrists.

"You mentioned a remit for high-risk research. What do you actually do here?" he asked.

Crowther stuck a label on each of the vials of blood as he spoke.

"Have you heard of MK Ultra?"

Blake shook his head.

"It was the code name for a secret US government research project through the CIA's scientific intelligence division. The aim was ambitious – to learn about the extent of human behavior through the investigation of mind control, behavior modification …" Crowther looked at Blake, his eyes narrowing. "Psychic ability. But alas, their methodologies meant the project was doomed once it became widely known what they were doing. They used drugs, isolation, torture and abuse on American citizens in the pursuit of knowledge. The aim was to give the USA an intelligence advantage, to create weapons that would target people's minds."

"Did they succeed?" Blake asked, tugging at his wrist restraint again, testing its strength.

"Officially, it was shut down, but of course, aspects continue under other names, other departments – using subjects that won't be missed, much as we do. But when our research found the correlation between mental health status and at least perceived psychic ability, we decided to continue investigation from another angle. What if the voices of schizophrenia are a form of extrasensory perception? What if the sensations of religious ecstasy are a form of mania? What if visions from God – or from the Devil – are just a higher function of the brain that we can all access?" Crowther's eyes were unblinking. A shiver ran down Blake's spine at the depth of his gaze, as if the man stripped away the flesh and bone on his face to see the mind within. He was no longer a person, just a vessel for a brain this man desired.

"Genealogy research is the next step, for if we can inter-breed those of you with these genetic gifts, we can create the mind-soldiers of the future, those who can work in the shadows of intelligence and return our country to the glory of Empire." Crowther placed the vials of blood into a plastic box and slipped it into his pocket. "Some of my colleagues see the mentally ill as dross to be bred out, but I want to sift through you all and find the hereditary gold." His eyes narrowed as he stepped towards the bed. Blake leaned back as Crowther loomed above him. "Your family is particularly special, Blake, and many of my colleagues are interested in trying their experiments out while you have your visions." He bent to the cabinet next to the bed, pulling out an electric razor. "But I get first crack, and we'll start as soon as the tequila poison is flushed from your system." Crowther switched on the razor, and pressed the button on the drip a few times, increasing the flow. "We'll need your head smooth for the equipment. Stay still now and this won't take long."

The buzzing filled Blake's mind and a cold sensation crept slowly up his arm from the drip. He tried to twist his head away but it was too heavy and his neck wasn't strong enough to move. As the drug-induced darkness descended, Blake heard Crowther begin to whistle softly as he worked.

CHAPTER 19

MARIE STEVENS PLACED HER leather-covered Bible on the narrow shelf in front of her, its beloved pages well-thumbed and marked with notes. She knelt on the embroidered cushion as the Reverend began to speak, his deep voice echoing through the nave of St Paul's Cathedral.

"Let us confess our sins in penitence and faith, firmly resolved to keep God's commandments and to live in love and peace with all."

Marie felt the impression of her knees snug on the cushion where so many of the faithful had knelt before, and it gave her comfort. She began the response, words she knew so well that she barely even registered them anymore at a conscious level. This was her ritual, the foundation of her week, and had been for the last forty-two years. She had sat in this cathedral with her parents, now beside God in Heaven, and she had met her husband here at one of the prayer groups. A fleeting uncharitable thought crossed Marie's mind, and she pushed it aside, offering her pain to Jesus.

"We look for the resurrection of the dead, and the life of the world to come. Amen."

Her weak ex-husband would get his just rewards in the hereafter. That was what Marie held onto during the lonely nights. That, and the touch of the Reverend's hand after the service, when briefly she felt his special blessing upon her.

Marie looked up towards the quire as the sun streamed in, a momentary glimpse of the holy here on Earth, a shimmering haze of gold dust illuminating divine miracle. In one alcove, Jesus was portrayed as crucified on the tree of life, the cross transformed by branches, leaves and a golden sun, with water running from the base in folds of blue and indigo, crested with gold. The sunlight picked out rich color on the wings of angels, the feathers of peacocks. Then, a cloud passed over and the moment slipped away.

The Reverend finished the prayers and took the Eucharist himself as the organ quietly played, encouraging a penitent calm. A line quietly formed, each waiting their turn for the Host as the faithful knelt at the altar. Marie walked slowly to the front, calming her heartbeat as she knelt again, hands cupped before her.

"The body of Christ," the Reverend intoned, placing the wafer in her hands.

"Amen," Marie whispered, meeting his eyes and then placing the wafer in her mouth.

"The blood of Christ," he said, and tipped a little wine between her lips. The chalice was cool on her mouth, and for a moment, Marie thought she felt the Reverend's fingers brush her neck.

The wine tasted unusual today, a little stronger than last week. It felt like fire down her throat, with a warming aftertaste, like a good whiskey. Marie said her silent prayer, thanking Jesus for his sacrifice. She stood and walked, head down, back to her pew where she knelt in contemplation for a moment. As she moved to sit up again, Marie's head began to spin. She reached out a hand to steady herself. She looked towards the altar and it seemed as if the gold from the mosaics had lifted off the walls and now rained down on the congregation. The painted Eden on the ceiling of the quire pulsated with energy, as if the garden would erupt with fecundity and spill down the walls, so they could dwell again with God in that holy place. It was beautiful, surely some kind of holy vision.

A single voice rang out in the quire, one of the choristers intoning a holy prayer. Unusual, but beautiful, Marie thought. She lifted her arms towards Heaven, prayers so fervent in her chest, she thought she would burst with joy. She noticed other people around her beginning to weep. Something was happening. Was this the outpouring of the spirit promised in the book of Acts?

Even as holy exultation welled up inside, Marie became aware of a malevolence behind her, a cold shadow that threatened to sweep over the congregation. She looked towards the back door of the cathedral and saw a darkness in the shadows where the sun could no longer reach. The people who sat there looked misshapen, deformed, and they were swaying and moaning. Marie sent up a prayer to Jesus, knowing in her heart that this was Satan attempting to stop the holy visions, trying to prevent the purposes of the Most High. But the Evil One must not prevail, could not prevail in this holy place.

As she looked to either side, Marie saw there were people nearer to her twisting into grotesque shapes, some bent double and vomiting as they morphed into their true demonic forms. Her eyes fell on an angel, standing with a scythe in the portico of a doorway. As she watched, it stepped down and began to swing the weapon, its face turning from heavenly contemplation into the visage of corruption, the promise of torture in its eyes. Marie knew it was a fallen one that wanted to take its victims to the depths of Hell, as company in the darkness and the agony of separation from God.

Marie watched in horror as undulations of other forms erupted from the stone around her. The monuments to the war heroes rippled with energy and figures with swords and knives awakened to seek victims around them. With muscled torsos and strong arms, they raised their weapons to bring long-dead vengeance to this place. Held captive for so long in stone tombs, they now rose again to smite those the Lord had decided to punish. The whispered prayers of the desperate caught in the ornate decorations, decaying as they rose, stuck on their journey to an uncaring God. The cross as the route to salvation became the instrument of torture once more and Marie watched as Jesus writhed in his death agonies.

Angels launched themselves from the dome, voices like a chorus of waterfalls, crashing into explosive sound. Birds of paradise flew out from the Eden above, their wings an iridescent blue, their song turned into a souring roar by the rasp of teeth in their beaks. Their blue feathers split open to reveal rotten black, their taloned feet poised ready to rip the flesh from the faithful. The sun that had been shining down in rays of gold now turned into streams of piss, stinking and dirty, the stench soaking the parishioners who twisted under its impurity. Marie clutched her hands together in prayer, whispering to herself. "'Even though I walk through the valley of the shadow of death, I will fear no evil, for you are with me.'"

A crash came from the altar as great candles were pushed to the floor by a choir that rampaged in righteous anger, beating the young boys who had turned into demonic hosts. As flames caught, smoke filled the air, shrouding the cathedral with a thick grey mist. Warped figures thrust out of the fog, talons clawing for more flesh to rip apart. Then Marie saw the Reverend, arms outstretched to his flock, his body transfigured as he bellowed words from the book of Daniel.

"'There before me was a fourth beast – terrifying and frightening and very powerful. It had large iron teeth; it crushed and devoured its victims and trampled underfoot whatever was left.'"

The Reverend's eyes were red and his skin crawled with maggots that burrowed into his flesh, making him an undead freak. The smell of rotting flesh filled the air, overlaid with the scent of incense as from a tomb. Marie heard a scream and realized it came from her own throat as she looked on his sickening visage, but hers was no longer a lone voice. Her shouts were part of a chorus of screams and moans that came from the thickening horde around her, as demons slithered from the cracks in the floor to torment the souls around her.

She watched two men pull a woman to the floor, one holding her down as the other pulled up her skirt. Marie could see demons cleaved to the backs of the men, their vicious mouths urging violence, long tongues licking at exposed flesh. The woman screamed, even as her mouth was smothered by a fearful creature with lizard frills about its neck and smoke rising from its back.

The organ sounded as a cacophony, polyphonic doom rippling through her skull, but it couldn't drown out the coughs of the evil ones, their throaty roars and hacking hate. Had God abandoned them to this evil? Or was this a test that Marie must overcome for Him to pour out His blessings again?

People around her had faces of demons now, their hands misshapen claws, stalking towards her to rip off her skin and eat her flesh. Marie had to stop them reaching her. She stood up on the pew, grabbing her Bible. She swung it down onto the head of what had once been a woman next to her. The thing fell to the floor, and as she opened her mouth, Marie saw a smaller demon inside, the jaw expanding to allow the fetid parasite to escape. Marie felt the wrath of God rise up inside her as she beheld the abomination of God's corrupted child. This would be her victory, this would be her offering to the Almighty. By vanquishing Satan, she would be able to sit at the right hand of God with Jesus and all the angels.

As the demon began to emerge, its body hairy and mis-shapen, Marie used the heavy Bible to beat at it with both hands. The wet thwack resonated through her, the weight of it sounding as a drum pulsing with the power of God. She felt the muscles in her arms tense, flooded with the strength of His army to vanquish the wicked and she heaved it against the woman's head again and again until blood and bone stained the leather Bible, a perfect sacrifice in this now-corrupted place.

BBC NEWS REPORT

The Christian community are holding prayer vigils throughout London tonight as nearly two hundred people were taken to hospital following an incident at St Paul's Cathedral during the afternoon service. Three fatalities have been reported, one from heart failure and two others from the brutal violence that broke out within the cathedral. Other injuries include trampling, shock, various degrees of physical trauma as well as poisoning. Five victims of rape have also been reported.

"The victims from St Paul's have tested positive for a strong psychoactive drug," Police Commissioner Malcolm Jordan said in a statement to the press. "It's thought to have been administered through the Communion wine and quickly brought on hallucinations that caused the outbreak of violence within the church."

Survivors who had not taken Communion say the cathedral had descended quickly into madness after the Eucharist was taken.

"It seemed as if some kind of collective madness took hold of most of the congregation," parishioner Eric Smythe explained. "I couldn't believe it at first, as some couples began to behave sexually and others with violence, in the middle of a sacred church service. Within a few minutes, it seemed certain that something was very wrong. That's when I called the police … The whole thing only lasted about fifteen minutes, but I will never forget what I saw in this church today."

CHAPTER 20

The clatter of metal instruments woke Blake and for a moment he didn't recognize where he was. His body was heavy, his mind a blur. As he remembered, he raised his arm, the restraints still locked on his wrists. Looking towards the end of the bed, he saw the chair with the head brace. That hadn't been his imagination. Crowther was setting up equipment and he glanced over as he heard Blake's movements.

"Good morning." The doctor was cheery, enthusiasm oozing from him.

"If it's such a good morning, how about unshackling me?" Blake tried.

Crowther smiled, his perfect teeth glistening. "It's actually a good morning for experimentation. For that, you need to remain restrained – for now." He licked his lips as he looked at Blake, as if about to swallow a tasty morsel of flesh. He pulled a plastic gown on over his white coat, the kind that would keep bodily fluids from staining his clothes, and then began to prep a syringe of pale green fluid.

"This will make you uncaring of shackles anyway, you'll be so lost in its embrace." Crowther tapped the syringe with a fingernail. "It's an amnesiac as well as – let's say, a mind relaxant. Something to deaden the prefrontal cortex, release the inhibitors to perception. You don't need drugs to see your visions, Blake, but this will intensify them, make them even more real. And whatever happens here, whatever horrors you experience, you'll only see them again in your nightmares." He hesitated a moment, his eyelids flickering. "Of course, some cannot separate the nightmare from reality but perhaps we can help you find some peace, Blake, some escape from the visions that torment you. But first, let's see how far they go."

Crowther advanced on the bed, and pushed the syringe into the cannula on Blake's shackled hand. Blake watched the green liquid as the plunger pushed it into his bloodstream. Part of him wanted to scream and jerk his body away, stop this drug from polluting him, but another side welcomed its embrace. For years he had wondered at his abilities. Perhaps this would help him push his ability to the limit and work out what it really was. If it didn't break his mind first.

Within a minute, the light in the room intensified. Blake could see every pore on Crowther's skin, every pixel of color in the man's heterochromic eyes. The sound of the air conditioner was heightened and he could hear his own heartbeat, steady and rhythmic. The overpowering smell of antiseptic made his nose wrinkle, and under it, he sensed a note of decay, a hint of something that had died here.

"Come and sit in the chair now. You'll find it very comfortable." Crowther unlocked the handcuffs and helped Blake from the bed into the reclining chair. A tiny part of Blake's mind saw a glimmer of escape, but it was smothered by a wonder of heightened sensation. What did his life matter when the world was so expansive, when he was just part of a grander whole? It was as if he had found his true place in the universe and he wanted to stay there forever.

Crowther rubbed a cold jelly on his shaven scalp and Blake shivered at the tendrils of pleasure that wound down his spine from the pressure. Crowther added a heavy mesh of electrodes in a skullcap. It seemed as if the world was in slow motion, and Blake felt anticipation rise in his belly at the thought of how his visions would be intensified. Crowther turned to the bench and opened a drawer. He pulled out a plain blue book, the edges worn.

"This is a family heirloom," he said, his fingers caressing the pages. "I know what it contains, but to prove the truth of your visions, I want you to tell me what you see."

Blake reached for the book, a tingling of expectancy in his scarred hands. He closed his eyes as he felt the weight of it in his palms and the veil of mist descended.

***

The smell of vomit and piss made him gag and Blake opened his eyes to find himself in a large room. A wooden apparatus was built around the walls and from it hung a chair. Strapped into the device was a young woman, her head lolling forward as she continued to puke and cough. Her clothes were dark with sweat, and between her legs, clear evidence that she had wet herself. Her hair was matted around her forehead, her eyes dull with pain. A man knelt next to her, lifting the woman's chin, making sure to avoid the mess around her mouth.

"Again," he said tersely, rising and walking away.

"No," she moaned. "Please, no."

From the side of the room, Blake heard a clack of gears and then the chair was raised. The woman lunged, trying to escape, but she was strapped firmly to it. The chair started to rotate, first in small circles and then it swung out as it revolved faster and faster.

"Another half an hour and she'll be a lot more docile," a voice behind him said.

Blake yanked his hand from the book, emerging once more into the pristine lab. He gasped, heart thumping at the peculiar torture of the woman and the implied threat of what awaited her afterward.

"What did you see?" Crowther asked, leaning close.

"Some kind of spinning device, a woman strapped into it." Crowther's smile was predatory, and Blake saw recognition in his eyes. "What is this book?"

"My ancestor, Bryan Crowther, was the surgeon at Bethlem Hospital between 1789 and 1815. The device you saw was known as rotational therapy, spinning the mad to induce vomiting, purging and vertigo. The book is his personal notebook of the experiments he did on the living – and the dead. Now, you must go back in. I want to know more."

Blake shook his head. "No, I don't want to see anything else."

He made to get up and Crowther moved swiftly, pushing him back down and using a strap to secure Blake's neck to the chair. Quickly, he secured Blake's hands to the arms and added a waist strap and ankle restraints.

"Then we'll just have to do this the hard way." Crowther placed the book under Blake's hand and wrapped a series of bandages around it, holding the pages against his bare skin. Blake fought the undertow of the visions, but the drug made his descent even faster. His eyelids flickered.

***

It was the smell of rotting flesh that greeted him this time, and Blake opened his eyes to find himself in a dark room lit only by a few candles. There were windows open to the night air but they did nothing to disguise the stench of the dead. A man was bent over a body on a gurney, focused on its head. With a knife, he cut around the forehead and peeled back the skin to reveal the skull. Blake sensed an echo of the anatomists he had encountered in the last case. He shuddered as the man picked up a saw and began to rasp the blade against the bone.

The man's breath was labored as he finished cutting through the skull and pried the bone cap off with a small flat bar, revealing the brain. With bare hands, he pulled the jelly-like organ out into a dish, cutting away the vessels that held it, and placed it on a wooden board. The man wiped his hands on his apron and scratched some notes into a book. He cut into the brain, picking up the chunks and examining them next to the candlelight. A smile twitched around his lips as he worked, and soon, the brain was reduced to mush on the bench. The man swept the pieces back into the dish, wiped his hands on a piece of linen next to the bench and walked to the next gurney. The body was covered with a sheet, only the head exposed, and Blake could see it was the young woman he had seen on the rotational device. The man picked up the knife and walked to the head of the gurney.

Suddenly, Blake saw the sheet twitch where the woman's fingers must be. The doctor stopped and pulled up the sheet, checking the straps around her wrists, making sure they were tight. He placed the knife down and returned to the bench, picking up the dirty strip of linen covered in pieces of brain. As the woman's eyes fluttered open, he wrapped the linen around her mouth as a gag. She moaned, an animal sound of terror.

"Don't struggle, my dear," the man whispered, as he picked up the knife again. "You'll be far more useful this way."

Blake tried to pull away from the vision, tried to drop through the veils of consciousness. He didn't want to watch this atrocity, but as the doctor began to cut across the

woman's face, he realized his hand was strapped to the book.
He couldn't leave until Crowther allowed him to, he had to
bear witness. As the doctor picked up the saw, Blake felt a
scream rise up within him.

CHAPTER 21

THE GALLERY WAS TUCKED into one of the hidden squares in the warren of back streets within the City of London. As she walked, Jamie tried to put Blake out of her mind in order to focus on the case. She still hadn't heard from him and she was worried, but then he was probably just curled up somewhere with a shocking hangover. Maybe someone lay by his side, and she definitely didn't want to dwell on that thought. He would answer his phone when he was ready, and she had enough to deal with right now. The murder at the cathedral was now complicated by the drugged wine and the motive for the murder of the Canon was clearly bound up in the hallucinogenic experience. But what was the point of sending those people mad? Now there was another murder, and the pressure to find a viable suspect was intense.

Morning commuters rushed past, most not even glancing at the police presence and crime-scene tape. Jamie wondered what could penetrate the armor of self-protection that Londoners assumed about them like a cloak. To survive here, city dwellers needed to let the news roll off their backs, remaining impervious despite the proximity of disaster. Selective perception was the only way to avoid going completely crazy with worry.

Missinghall munched on his second cheese and ham croissant, brushing crumbs from his suit jacket as they walked towards the cordoned-off area.

"Posh place," he said. "Guess this lot can afford this sorta thing."

"Art not your bag, Al?"

Missinghall smiled broadly. "Only the kind on a beer label."

His humor soon dimmed as they approached the crime scene. They suited up in protective clothing and signed into the log, checking the protocol with officers present. They walked into the glass-fronted gallery to see a few large canvases, all modern art, completely bereft of any realism. Exactly the kind of work that would sell in this area, Jamie thought, for anyone could project their own interpretation onto the canvas. The city thrived on the scramble for personal success, and art was still a reflection of wealth, even in these days of supposed austerity. Perhaps especially now.

Jamie smelled the body before they saw it, resonant of roasted pork and not unpleasant if you didn't know what it implied. They walked into the back room of the gallery where forensic pathologist Mike Skinner was still processing what he could of the body in situ.

A man was firmly tied to a sturdy chair, in a straitjacket with crossed arms strapped to the opposite sides. Next to the chair was a black box with leads that connected to electrodes on the man's closely shaven scalp. There were burns on either side of his head, the source of the roasted-meat smell in the air. Blood had dried around his mouth and there were spots of burgundy on the straitjacket.

Skinner lifted his head from the examination, seeing Jamie and Missinghall.

"The body was discovered by the gallery owner's assistant when she came in this morning to open up. The deceased is Arthur Tindale, owner of the gallery." Not known for his small talk, Skinner's tone was efficient and to the point. "I'll need to check for certain at the lab, but I'd say cause of death was electrocution." Skinner gestured to the box next to the chair. "This is an old device, originally used in electroshock therapy for mental illness, but the safety levels have been altered to produce a deadly voltage." Skinner shook his head. "It wasn't a quick death." He pointed to the mouth of the victim. "The blood is from where he bit his tongue during the shocks. This man was tortured with smaller doses before the voltage was taken up so high that his heart stopped."

Electroconvulsive Therapy (ECT) had been used to treat severe depression, mania and schizophrenia since the 1940s. Jamie knew that these days it was delivered with muscle relaxants, but that there was still possible memory loss and other side effects. Despite claims of medical efficacy for major depression, the public impression was tainted by visions of death-row inmates in the electric chair and portrayals in films and literature. Indeed, Ernest Hemingway had committed suicide shortly after receiving ECT, his famous description of the experience: "It was a brilliant cure but we lost the patient." This murder was about madness yet again, Jamie thought, but what was the gallery owner's connection with Monro, or the Canon at the cathedral?

"Three makes a serial killer," Missinghall said quietly, with an inappropriate tinge of excitement in his voice. Serial killers were rare, despite the intensity of media and myriad fictional characters, and they had never had a case on their team. Jamie shook her head.

"I don't think we should go down that path yet, because of the media hype it will create. There's a connection between these murders, for sure. But they aren't random, and these deaths seem to be personal, so I don't think the general public is at risk. The question must be whether the murderer is finished yet, and what Arthur Tindale did to be targeted."

One of the Scene of Crime Officers dusted the electroshock machine for prints, but Jamie suspected the scene would be as clean as the Imperial War Museum and the crypt of St Paul's.

"You can get those machines on eBay," Missinghall said, looking up from his smartphone. "Maybe we can track down someone who bought one recently."

Jamie nodded. "Definitely worth following up." She walked over to the desk now that the SOCOs had finished processing it. "And we need to know what Tindale's link with madness was. Can you get something on his background, Al?"

Missinghall nodded and turned away to start making calls. Jamie looked down at the papers strewn on the desk, not touching anything, just processing Arthur Tindale's personal space. It was chaotic, but clearly organized in his own particular way. This was a man who actively ran his business, and who cared about the art he chose for his space, not just the income it brought.

There was a mockup of a brochure on the top of one of the piles, and the striking front image caught Jamie's eye. It showed a giant skull, bisected so the viewer could see into compartments that made up the interior of the brain. Jamie bent to look closer at the incredible detail of each mini tableau. In one cell, a woman was gagged and tied to a pole as a man whipped her back, blood pooling at her feet. In another, a tiny girl was trapped inside a spiky horse chest-nut, but the spines pointed inwards, piercing her body and holding her prisoner, each movement ripping open her bare flesh. Yet another compartment showed a sickly, albino rat cowering in a dark corner, baring its teeth. There was a man strapped to a conveyor belt heading for a crushing set of rollers. The same figure beat on the glass walls of a test tube as giant scientists hovered, ready to pour a vial of pale green liquid over their subject. Creatures crawled around the edges of the painting, some recognizable as worms and lizards, but others fantastical nightmares, chimaeras of horror, and each was biting at the skull, trying to burrow inside.

With a gloved hand, Jamie turned the brochure over. The painting was called *Labyrinth* but there was no name of the artist shown. She glanced around the gallery again, but she knew the painting wasn't there. The piece was stunning, and she would have noticed it as they walked in.

There was an empty space on the wall opposite where the body had been secured. In a gallery with so few paintings, it seemed strange that the area had been left unadorned and Arthur Tindale would have died gazing at that exact spot.

"Al, can you find out whether there was any artwork on this wall? The assistant should know."

Missinghall nodded, getting his phone out of his pocket. "She's still with a female officer going over her statement. I'll find out."

Jamie looked around the office space, but there seemed to be no obvious records of the artists and their work. After the SOCOs had finished, they would be able to process all this paperwork. She looked down again. The painting disturbed her, and she recognized something of the colors in it.

Missinghall caught her eye as he finished his phone call, his face serious.

"You're right. There was a painting in that space yesterday. It was called *Labyrinth*. The artist was Lyssa Osborne."

"We need to find Matthew," Jamie said, remembering the look on his face when he had talked about his sister. She glanced at her watch. "His Bill on mental health is due to be debated later, but if we go straight to his flat, we should just catch him."

CHAPTER 22

THE RAIN BEGAN AS Matthew Osborne reached the gates of Kensal Green Cemetery. He lifted his head to taste the first drops, remembering the tip of Lyssa's chin and her laugh as she used to do just that. She had loved the rain, and the sound of it calmed her even in the rollercoaster of mania. He had installed a skylight in her bedroom so she could listen to the rain at night, the lull of it soothing her to sleep. Now, he let the water trickle down inside the collar of his coat, wanting the sensation of cold fingers on his spine, wanting to shiver. Anything to feel again.

Matthew walked through the graveyard, accustomed to the path now, the tombs familiar sentinels on his routine visits. He wanted to talk to Lyssa once more, now that his course was set. Finally, there would be justice.

In the maelstrom of his plans and the deaths of those who had betrayed the mad, he still found peace here, a haven for the dead and the people who loved them. It was one of London's oldest graveyards, and the resonance of emotions tied to the dead remained, hovering, brooding.

Matthew looked up at the struts of the gas works behind the cemetery, like the ribs of a skinless drum, a skeleton of a building that looked down upon these many dead. He walked down the wide boulevard, past the rows of graves jostling for real estate in the crowded space. Kensal Green Cemetery was an eclectic mixture of historic graves, faded names etched with dates of years past and new monuments with garish colors and kitsch ornaments. Matthew looked down at one tomb, decorated with the wet remains of tinsel and a garden gnome dressed as Santa Claus. In many cultures, the living came to eat and party at the graveside, sharing food and wine in memory of those who had passed on. In London, those cultures sat side by side with the British sense of decorum and repression of emotion, the hidden depths of grief smothered by a downcast look and silent tears.

The newly dead still had people to mourn them, but Matthew knew that the majority were forgotten within three generations. People said they lived on through their children, but that was just genetics, nothing else. Most people left no trace upon the earth. Many didn't even know the names of their great grandparents, but his Lyssa deserved more than this silent grief, and today he would wreak havoc in her memory.

He stared at the rows of graves, a dominance of crosses against the pale blue sky, interspersed with melancholic angels. Was it all about legacy in the end? Only deeds remain, as our bodies disappear into the earth, rotting away. Whatever the truth, Matthew found peace here, as he had always done in graveyards. Back in the days when their parents fought after too many drinks, he and Lyssa used to sneak off to the nearby churchyard. He would recite to her from the graves, teaching her to read that way and the old-style lettering became her favorite font in later life. They had stayed there late into the night sometimes, curled up and sheltered from the wind by the heavy stones and cradled in the lush grass on the older graves. Sometimes they slept there, and Matthew remembered waking early one morning, in the first rays of sun. He had looked down at his sister's blonde hair, her long eyelashes against perfect skin and he had vowed to do anything to protect her.

He passed the grand graves either side of the main walkway, the most expensive plots in this fight for celestial real estate. Those inside were all the same in death, rotting corpses with memorials tattooed in platitudes. He 'fell asleep,' she 'rests in peace,' they all 'sleep with the angels.' Everyone was described in glowing terms: beloved husband, devoted wife, perfect father, true friend. There were no sinners in the graveyard, all were cleansed of individual personality, reduced to a name, a date and the relationship to those who buried them.

Matthew walked on through the riot of stone crosses, gravestones and small monuments. Nature was on the edge of reclaiming this land, tendrils of ivy growing up around the feet of the angels, moss on the roof of the mausoleum, the cracking tombstones and listing monuments, sinking into the earth. The limbs of trees stretched out like a blessing, shielding their charges from the rain above, the noise on the stones a soft drip. He passed a grave with an inscription from Revelation: *God will wipe every tear from their eyes. There will be no more death or mourning or crying or pain, for the old order of things has passed away. I am making everything anew.* Matthew felt a strengthening of his resolve, for he had only to go forward now. To pave the way for a new order of understanding, he had to destroy the old order, and God wasn't the only one who could accomplish that. He reached out to touch an angel guarding a tomb, a gesture he found himself repeating every visit. The angel stood in a modest pose, head and eyes down, wings folded, hands clasped with a wreath between her fingers. Behind its watchful gaze, his sister lay sleeping.

Her stone was modest. *Lyssa, Beloved Sister.* Nothing more, for that defined her on this earth in his eyes. Her art had been but an outpouring of her name: mad, crazy goddess. Matthew knelt by the plain granite headstone, next to the mound of earth that marked the recent grave. He imagined her precious body beneath the dark soil, the worms that curled between her ribs, the insects that ate her flesh. It didn't matter, for her physical body had never been the remarkable thing about her. It was her mind that had soared above mere mortals.

Reaching into his pocket, Matthew pulled out a slim paperback. Lyssa had loved to read, loved to perform, so he still brought her books. There were other rain-sodden texts here, the remains of words that dripped ink into her grave, trickling through the earth to write his love on her corpse.

"Oh, for a muse of fire," Matthew whispered as he laid down a new volume, the words from Shakespeare's *Henry V*, the last play they had seen together. It had become his regular prayer, for she had been his muse, and now her light was gone. But he still had time to make others see as she had.

"It worked, Lyssa," he whispered, patting a little of the earth back into place, as he placed the book on her grave. "The drug worked, and the sane became moonstruck in St Paul's. The effects are long lasting, and my hope is that some of them won't ever return to mundanity but will stay in that other place." He bent to stroke her headstone, his voice full of regret. "You know that other place, you chose it over me after all. Now it's time to finish what I started and I'll be with you soon enough."

Matthew stood, looking down at the plot next to her. The double headstone was only half filled with her name, the space for his still empty. The mason had refused to carve it, calling it bad luck to inscribe a name while he was still living. Matthew felt an almost overwhelming compulsion to lie down next to Lyssa's grave, to coat himself in the earth that covered her. He desired only to lie in peace with her now, but there was one thing left to finish.

A massive sepulcher squatted behind Lyssa's grave, a giant stone edifice with letters carved in its side. *Dominus dedit. Dominus abstulit.* The Lord gives and the Lord takes away. The words were from Job, the story of a man tortured by Satan, while God allowed his faith to be tested. The sepulcher's main door had been sealed when the last of the family had been laid to rest here a generation ago, but in the recent storms the ground under the tomb had subsided. The strain on the door had cracked the entrance and Matthew had managed to lever it open.

Looking around to check no one was nearby, he removed the crowbar from his rucksack and went to the door of the mausoleum. Gently, he pried it open, slipping behind it into the dark. The space smelled of damp earth, and the bodies that had once lain here were dust long ago. The dead were not the ones to fear, anyway; this graveyard was far safer than the housing estates just down the road, where violence terrorized children as once it had him and Lyssa. Here there was only quiet, the soft patter of rain on leaves and stone outside, the sounds that would outlast all who visited here.

Matthew pulled a camping lantern from his pack and switched it on, the fluorescent bulb lighting the inside of the tomb. For all its exterior ornate decoration, inside was just a rack of shelves covered in the dust of corpses. A whisper of memory lingered here and Matthew was careful not to disturb what remained.

He bent down, kneeling on the floor. He reached under the bottom shelf, feeling his way to the back, and pulled out a small case, the type that could hold a musical instrument. The type that you wouldn't think of questioning in this city of ultimate acceptance. He opened it to reveal ten test tubes and two empty spots for the vials he had used at St Paul's. Plenty left for what he planned today.

CHAPTER 23

WALKING ACROSS WESTMINSTER BRIDGE, the sun warm on his skin, Matthew smiled. A champagne fizz thrummed in his veins, anticipation of what was to come. Today was the Second Reading of his proposed Bill on changes to the Mental Health Act in the House of Commons. Today, he was supposed to debate the merits of the clauses with those Ministers who cared enough to speak. But Matthew knew the truth. There was no way this Bill would go any further, no way that the media and the public would find out what he wanted, what he needed them to know. There were too many who protected their own interests, who had constituents that were more powerful, lobbying groups that wanted the mentally ill to disappear and stop being a drain on taxpayers' money. Even when most of the mentally ill were taxpayers anyway.

Christian Monro's research had galvanized support for extreme right-wing views, meaning that this Bill, generous to those in need, would be quashed by stronger voices than his. But the Bill would make the news tonight, Matthew would make sure of that, and the politicians who scoffed at the mentally ill might finally experience a slice of their pain.

He looked up at the Palace of Westminster, the cool stone blessed by sunlight. He never failed to be in awe of its grandeur. The Elizabeth Tower, named Big Ben after its bell, towered above the Thames, its clock face marking time for the nation. Originally a medieval palace, the buildings had been destroyed by fire a number of times and the present design had been constructed in the mid-nineteenth century. The Gothic architecture was dominated by vertical lines, as if a giant beast had raked its claws down the outside of the building, anchoring the spires to the banks of the river that nurtured the great city of London. Matthew dodged around the tourists on the bridge, understanding their need to capture its architectural beauty. This was his city, and pride swelled his throat as he glanced east towards the London Eye, the Shard and onwards, imagining the Thames Barrier and the ocean beyond.

London had always been a refuge for those on the perimeter of society, and every kind of outsider could find a niche in its maelstrom. Those who didn't fit into provincial towns could lose themselves here in anonymity, those rejected as wrong somehow could be welcomed into a community. There was a place for all here, but Westminster didn't truly represent the people of London. It still stood for the elite, those who sat above the marginalized and judged them for what they didn't have and couldn't get. Matthew had tried to break through the barriers of class and attitude, but the group he represented had too many disparate voices, weakened by years of their own suffering. They were too busy trying to survive each day, and couldn't spare the energy to convince others they were worthy of higher regard. But today these men of power – and they were mostly men – would understand.

Matthew approached the Parliament entrance for MPs and other regular visitors, and pulled the small rucksack from his shoulder, readying himself for the security protocol. The area was set up like an airport, with clearance machines for bags and a metal detector to walk through. He exhaled to try and control his fast heartbeat.

"Good morning, Jen." He smiled at the middle-aged security guard who worked here most mornings.

"Is it a good one?" Jen frowned, exhaustion evident in her stance and a dullness in her eyes.

"Are you alright?" Matthew asked, part of him desperate to run past her as fast as possible, but holding himself back. He was known to be a bit chatty in the mornings, more friendly than most of the MPs who rushed by, oblivious to those who served them.

"Sean, one of my kids, is ill. I was up all night with him." Jen ran the rucksack through the detector, and Matthew tried not to pay attention to it, keeping his face concerned for her as he stepped through the archway with no problems.

"That's a shame. I hope he gets better soon." The baggage machine beeped. "Oh, I'm sorry," Matthew said, his face suitably apologetic. "It's my flask again, you know it always sets the bloody machine off."

Jen pulled the rucksack out and opened it for him. Matthew took out the metal flask, its matte silver surface reflecting a distorted version of his face.

"I don't know why you don't just use a plastic one," Jen said. "It would save all this nonsense. I swear we go through this way too often." She paused. "Unless you're just angling for some extra time with me."

Matthew laughed along with her, trying not to make her comment too much of a joke, even as he noted her grey hair and bulging uniform.

"Chemicals in plastic ..."

"Get into the water," she finished for him. "Yeah, I know." She shook her head. "As if we don't already have way too much to worry about." She handed him the flask. "Enjoy your day, Mr Osborne."

The flask was cool in Matthew's hand, an innocuous container within which judgement sat waiting.

***

Matthew walked through the grand building towards the Churchill Room. He had arranged for a reception before the Second Reading debate and as it was after lunch, he knew the Members would likely have a few drinks. You didn't become an MP without being able to hold your alcohol, and fortifying oneself for an afternoon debate was a pleasurable way to drift easily through the rest of the day. He passed a few other MPs in the hallway, nodding to them but not stopping. Matthew put on the air of a man worried about his fortunes in the hours ahead, and he knew that people wanted to avoid talking anyway. They all expected his Bill to be kicked out. After all, he'd only made it to the Second Reading by calling in some favors, and today was his last chance to be heard.

The Members' Lobby was empty, a moment of calm before the MPs arrived en masse for the afternoon debate. Matthew checked his pigeon hole. It amused him that these archaic wooden boxes were still used in an age of instant connection through email and social media. Perhaps the post boxes were only used for the romantic trysts that everyone knew went on inside the nooks and crannies throughout the palace, behind the faded grandeur. Power was ever an aphrodisiac.

Matthew turned into the Churchill Room, the paintings of previous Ministers looking down with superiority onto the long tables set out for the reception.

"Everything ready, Peter?"

Peter Jensen looked up from polishing glasses on the table in front of him, making sure there were no spots to be seen. "Just the wine to bring through, Mr Osborne."

London's hard water made it difficult to ever get glass crystal clear, but Peter seemed to manage it. He had been a steward at Westminster for many years and Matthew had fostered a friendship with him, enlisting his help for a number of events. Part of him worried about the old man today, whether he would be blamed for what would happen. He pushed those thoughts aside.

"Oh, I can get that," Matthew said, as Peter made to put down the glass he polished. "You finish the glasses. Don't let me interrupt."

"I've decanted some of the better stuff from your selection." There was a mischievous twinkle in Peter's eye, a nod to the snobbery of the wine elite.

Matthew smiled. "Thanks. I need all the help I can get this afternoon."

He slipped out through a door that led into an anteroom. A couple of the waitresses bustled around with canapés at one end of the room, but they barely gave him a glance as they were so engrossed in gossip. Matthew went to the wine table, slipping off his rucksack and pulling the flask out. With his back blocking any view of what he was doing, Matthew grasped one of the vials and poured a generous amount into a couple of the decanters. He needed to work quickly, as Peter didn't have too many more glasses to polish. The chatter of the girls continued, but Matthew was hyper-aware of their presence, his heart hammering at the thought of being interrupted.

There were ten other bottles of wine open on the table, their contents breathing. He checked the labels, all excellent wines he had ordered for the occasion. Working quickly, Matthew dribbled a little of the vials into each bottle. It was a much larger dose than St Paul's, but then, that had been a dry run, and this was the real thing.

He heard the voices behind him change volume, turning

towards him perhaps, wondering what he was doing. He grabbed a cloth and wiped the rim of the final bottle, slipping the material over the flask as he turned to face the approaching waitresses.

"I'll take these in to Peter," he said, voice measured. "Thank you ladies, for all you do to help."

The girls smiled and turned to go back towards the kitchens.

As soon as they left the room, Matthew packed the empty vials into the flask, put it back in his pack, and pushed it under the table. He picked up two decanters and started to carry them out into the main room, just as Peter came in.

Matthew smiled. "I was just chatting with the girls," he said, handing Peter the decanters. "You take those and I'll bring the other bottles."

CHAPTER 24

JAMIE LOOKED AROUND MATTHEW Osborne's flat, remembering how she had sat with him here, an echo of the love for his sister a fleeting thought through her mind. They had been briefly united in grief, but he had used the emotion to blind her to his true plans. How could she not have seen that other facet of his personality? The side that wanted revenge and justice. The side that she had shown herself in the fiery labs of West Wycombe.

"Where should we start looking?" Missinghall asked, standing in the middle of the room, his large frame filling the space. As they both pulled on sterile gloves, Jamie thought back to the conversation when she had been here last. Matthew had indicated that she sit on the sofa and he had sat opposite in the green easy chair, its springs sagging in the middle, the once-rich colors faded.

"We need to get into his mind," Jamie said, as she walked over and sat down in the green chair. "I think he used to sit here most often." She leaned forward at an angle and put her hand down by the side of the chair, grinning as she sat back up, a worn copy of Shakespeare's *Hamlet* in her hand, its slim leather cover decorated with intricate swirls.

"'The balance of his mind is lost,'" Jamie whispered, looking at the cover, remembering a line from a long-ago English class.

Missinghall shook his head. "I've never seen it, but I presume Hamlet was mad? There seems to be a lot of that going round at the moment."

Jamie tilted her head on one side. "The play also contains the suicide of Ophelia, and the theme of madness runs through *Hamlet* like a thread of tainted blood."

"Seems entirely appropriate for Matthew Osborne to be reading it then," Missinghall said. "Perhaps he sees himself as some kind of tragic hero."

Jamie thumbed through the pages. "Look at this. It's dog-eared and some of the text is worn away towards the edges where his thumbs would rest. He was clearly obsessed with this book." She paused, shaking her head a little. "I just didn't see the depth of his infatuation with Lyssa and her suicide."

"It's not your fault, Jamie," Missinghall said. "None of us thought he was a serious suspect. He's an MP, for a start, and he has that charity thing. The guy's a model citizen."

Jamie's gaze fell on the wall where Lyssa's striking canvases hung. Matthew would have looked at them while sitting in this chair reading, a permanent reminder of his loss. What if he had something else there, too?

"Help me take those down," Jamie said, pointing at the paintings.

Together they lifted the first canvas from the wall to reveal smooth plaster behind it. As Jamie put it on the ground, she saw the back was marked by a bloody footprint and a scrawled message in looped handwriting.

"'Our vain blows malicious mockery,'" she read.

"Let me guess. *Hamlet* again?" Missinghall said as he grasped the edge of the second canvas.

Jamie nodded. "It's from the beginning of the play, when a ghost appears on the battlements of the castle in Denmark. The guards try to strike at the shade, but their swords pass through, making a mockery of their attempt – fighting fate can only ever be futile." An echo of Polly's death rippled through Jamie, and she understood Matthew's loss anew.

"Are you OK? Do you want to stop?" Missinghall asked, and Jamie saw empathy in his eyes.

"No, let's get this done."

They lifted together and put the second canvas on the floor next to the first. There was an alcove in the wall behind, a shadowed niche. Jamie lifted a fat sheaf of papers from the space, held together by a thin, brown folder. She carried it to the table and laid it down carefully so no papers would escape. She opened the file and flicked through a few pages, noting the chapter headings.

"It's Monro's book," she whispered, looking up at Missinghall. "The manuscript he was going to publish. It's his advice to the government on resuming sterilization of the mentally ill, on aggressive restraint for those committed and the resumption of the death penalty for those convicted of violent crime, specifically the criminally insane."

Missinghall exhaled with a whistle. "That stuff would have got Monro on every talk show in the country."

"Look at the symbol on the pages," Jamie said. "The book is sponsored by RAIN." She read from the text, "'The mad are monstrosities and tainted creatures.'"

Jamie turned another page to see a picture of Timothy MacArnold's grinning face, his arm raised to display the glitter of embedded diamonds. The reflected sparkle in his eyes was calculated to make the viewer judge him as maniacal. The following pages were a handwritten scrawl of notes, quotes from Timothy that he had thought would make him a superstar, but it looked like he had been digging his own grave.

Turning the pages further, Jamie found a case study of physical punishment as a treatment for mental illness and then a series of family trees with symbols for what Monro had labeled as degeneracy.

"'Three generations of idiots are enough,'" Missinghall

read from the text over her shoulder, an account of Buck vs Bell,1927, after which compulsory sterilization had been introduced in the US.

"This policy was Hitler's inspiration for his own eugenics program," Jamie said, remembering the horrors of Mengele, the Auschwitz angel of death hacking away at the bodies of his live subjects. She turned another page.

"Oh," she said with a sigh, unable to keep revulsion from her voice, as she saw what Monro had done to Lyssa Osborne. The series of photographs showed the young woman in various restraints. Her drugged eyes were glazed and staring, and a line of drool dripped from her mouth. She sat on the bench in Monro's private study, the box of sexual sadism sitting in plain view.

Jamie looked down at the canvases, what remained of Lyssa's vitality and passion for color. She thought of the vibrant woman dancing, her eyes bright with joy as she created, and what Monro had turned her into.

"I don't blame Osborne for wanting revenge," Missinghall said in a quiet tone, his large hands gentle on the page, his gloved fingers tracing Lyssa's face.

"That's the problem with this job," Jamie said. "Sometimes even murder is totally understandable. But this still isn't conclusive evidence of Matthew's responsibility for Monro's murder, and there's nothing here to link him to the gallery owner or the cathedral." Jamie was silent for a moment as she considered the options. "He's got to be at the Houses of Parliament right now, so I need you to go babysit, Al. I'll stay here and continue to go through this paperwork. See if I can find something we can clearly arrest him for, and in the meantime, you can keep an eye on him. Make sure he stays put."

"Sounds like a plan," Missinghall said. "I haven't been in the Houses of Parliament since I was a kid on a school trip. I'll text you when I'm there."

***

After a short journey across town, Missinghall quickened his pace as he strode towards the Churchill Room. The officers at the entrance had let him in based on his warrant card and a phone call to Detective Superintendent Cameron, but he was under clear orders to only observe for now. This was such a high-profile group of people that the consequences would be extreme if they had it wrong, especially before such an important Reading of the Bill. Missinghall's hand touched the outside of his pocket for the third time, checking that his phone was still there. Until there was word from Jamie of clear evidence to arrest Matthew Osborne, he would just have to wait. Missinghall looked up at the grand tapestries and the intricate wall carvings as he walked past, and smiled. This wasn't such a bad place to hang out in the meantime.

The door to the Churchill Room was open, and the hubbub of people talking spilled out into the corridor, voices lubricated by just enough alcohol to keep them going through the afternoon session. Missinghall stepped inside the reception room and stood against the wall, taking in the scene. He caught sight of Matthew Osborne deep in conversation with several Members of Parliament. There was a strange sense of recognizing these people from the media, of knowing snippets of their lives, but of course, they were just like anyone else in person. Pulling out his phone, Missinghall texted Jamie. *Am on scene at drinks reception.*

A young woman in a black and white uniform approached with a tray of canapés.

"Smoked salmon terrine, or venison carpaccio with fig," she said, offering the platter and a napkin. There was an answering pang in Missinghall's stomach as he surveyed the delicious tiny bites. It couldn't hurt to have a couple – after all, he might be here for a while and it was almost time for afternoon tea. He took a couple of each, popping one in his mouth. It was usually just a Rich Tea biscuit on the job, so these were too good to miss.

As the young woman walked away, a waiter took her place, holding a bottle of red wine with a splendid label that Missinghall knew he and the Missus would never see down their local.

"Can I interest you in this vintage, sir?"

The waiter held the bottle slightly tipped over a bulbous glass. Missinghall's mouth was full of glorious venison, so he could only nod slightly, realizing he needed something to wash down the food. He didn't drink much and it wasn't officially allowed on duty, but a few sips would surely be allowable, if only to blend into the crowd and keep an eye on Matthew Osborne. The waiter poured a generous measure, the wine swilling around and coating the sides of the glass.

"Thanks," Missinghall said, as he finished swallowing the canapé. He took a tiny sip as the waiter moved on. They had some good stuff, these MPs, he thought as the blackberry aftertaste filled his senses. He took another larger mouthful as he surveyed the room.

***

Matthew Osborne looked at his watch again. Only twenty minutes to go before they needed to move into the Chamber and only half the MPs were here. The Prime Minister still hadn't arrived, even though Matthew had followed up with his secretary this morning. At least those who were present were partaking of his generosity. They all knew the politics of the pre-debate reception, but all were disciples of Janus, the two-faced god, and they managed their betrayal with a glass of wine in hand. Matthew felt sweat drip down his back, sliding along his spine to pool where his shirt tucked into his suit trousers.

Suddenly, there was a ripple of conversation at the entranceway and Matthew saw Glen Abrahams enter the room, his trademark 'interested' face on. It drew people in and made them feel special, but for only a second before he moved on. The Prime Minister was a pro at working the room, fascinating to watch in action and Matthew couldn't help but admire the man, as much as he despised his individualist politics. Matthew walked to the drinks table, nodding at Peter to pour a glass from the special bottle of Bolney Estate Pinot Noir he had purchased especially for Abrahams. He knew the man was a stickler for all things British, part of his own insecurity as the child of an Eastern European immigrant family.

"Glen, thanks for coming," Matthew said as Abrahams approached, his eyes unreadable.

"Sorry to be late, Matthew. You know how it is. Are you ready for this debate? Great Bill, by the way. I know how much work you've put into it." For a moment, Matthew felt the effects of the distortion field Abrahams seemed to exude. Everyone did what the man wanted. Matthew held out the glass of red, his hand unwavering.

"You have to try this one. It's from Bolney Estate in Sussex, part of their new batch of pinot noir. I know Madeleine enjoys pinot, perhaps you can introduce her to a new one."

Abrahams took the glass, raised it to his nose and inhaled deeply. He waited the appropriate amount of time before giving his verdict.

"Umm, does smell good." He took a mouthful, swallowing it straight down. Matthew lifted his own glass, pretending to take a sip but barely allowing the liquid to touch his lips.

"That's so smooth. Lovely. Now, I must talk to Harriet before the debate starts. Please excuse me, Matthew, and all the best today."

Matthew saw the defeat that faced him in Abrahams' eyes, but it didn't matter anymore. He watched as the Prime Minister walked over to talk to Harriet Arbuthnot, MP for York Central, and continued to sip at the wine, draining the glass as the two spoke.

Within a few minutes the room started to clear as the MPs began to head towards the Chamber, ready for the debate.

"Good luck," Peter whispered, as he walked past with two of the empty decanters. Matthew smiled and nodded at him. It was time.

CHAPTER 25

WITH MISSINGHALL ON SCENE keeping an eye on Matthew Osborne, Jamie continued to search through the pile of papers. Amongst the typed manuscript pages, she found one in Lyssa's handwriting, torn from the notebook that Osborne had given her.

I know what Monro has done with my body. I feel the after-effects of his violation even though I'm not in myself as he does it. He's a vampire for the experiences of madness. He scribbles like he is the maniac as I speak of the things he wants to hear. If he could only see himself as he records my crazy, he would be the one under scrutiny. I've suggested he try certain drugs, to alter his own reality but he shakes his head violently, like a dog shaking off droplets of water. I don't think he trusts his own mind. As well he shouldn't, for when I glimpse the edge of my own consciousness, I realize that I'm not in control at all and shades of onyx and ebony begin to curl through my head.

Sometimes the darkness steals out of my brain at night, leaking out onto the pillow like quicksilver, and the shape shifter turns my world into a nightmare. I dream of Saturn devouring his son, the headless body clutched in bony hands as teeth tear another chunk from dead flesh. Wild hair and mad eyes fixed on my own as he swallows, ripping another mouthful, blood dripping down his chin, driven mad by the need to destroy that which he loves. Goya painted it on the walls of his own house, the Black Paintings. That is what he saw in the night, that is his legacy.

My own black paintings were formed in the house of RAIN, for now I know who they are, now I know what they did to me. Any chance I had to rise above my flawed chemistry is dashed, and they tore apart what remained. The strands that once held are now loose and broken. They said they would help me end it, that I wouldn't even have to lift my own hand. They will make it a celebration, and I welcome the finality.

But Matthew, oh, my brother. There's too much to say and not enough time. I am your smashed, damaged sister and you have forever been my champion. Your whole life has been tied to mine, like the tail of a kite, unable to escape following behind my ducking and diving. Never able to live for yourself, and defined by my broken life. By cutting us apart, I can set you free, as well as myself. Sometimes in your eyes I see a need to devour me, as if by making me a part of your body, you can make me whole. But sometimes you can't fix everything, and I'm so tired.

Jamie felt the prick of tears as she read Lyssa's final words, both for the woman who was lost and the brother intent on revenging her death. She understood the pull of violence in pursuit of justice, but Matthew had to be stopped. All she needed was clear evidence they could arrest him with and it had to be here somewhere. Jamie walked upstairs into the main office, determined to find it.

The upstairs room was spacious, a double bedroom turned into a workspace. After the riot of color on the walls downstairs, the palette here was somber. There were some hand weights and kettle-bells in one corner, and a Swiss ball instead of a desk chair. A wall calendar etched with black marker and highlighted sections betrayed how busy

Matthew usually was, but the months ahead were strangely empty, as if cleared of commitments. The room smelled fresh, notes of pine forest and spice in the air.

Jamie walked to the bookshelves, her eyes scanning for anything curious. There were a number of chemistry textbooks and journals with a thin hardback book next to them. She pulled the little book down and opened the front page. It was a Master's degree thesis on entheogens – psychoactive substances used in a spiritual context for transcendence and revelation. Osborne had once been a chemist. Jamie's mind leapt through the possibilities, the threads of the case entwining. Her heart thumped as she thought of Missinghall in the drinks reception at Westminster.

"Don't drink, Al," Jamie whispered, her voice a plea, as she grabbed her phone, dialing Missinghall's number. It rang and rang before clicking into voicemail. Perhaps he couldn't answer within the halls of Westminster. Perhaps he had already taken a sip. She texted him, her fingers mashing at the keyboard in her haste. *Osborne is the poisoner. Don't drink anything. Get security in there right now.*

She called again. No response. There was so little time, and she had to get to Missinghall. Jamie weighed up her options. Westminster was only a couple of blocks away. It would be quicker to get there herself and explain in person, rather than call and wait for the various approvals to go through. She turned quickly to head back downstairs. As she did so, her elbow knocked against another book. It dropped to the floor and a sheaf of photos fell out.

Jamie knelt down, gloved fingers pulling the pictures together briskly to tidy the scene. But something in them stopped her. They were stills of surveillance footage, showing figures entering and leaving a door under a series of railway arches, recognizable as an area near London Bridge station. One photo was dog-eared, and Jamie pulled it from the pack. The street lamps lit up the face of Lyssa Osborne, the date stamp just a few days before her death. Two men flanked her, either helping her in or making sure she entered. This must be the RAIN clinic Lyssa had referred to. Matthew had been keeping surveillance on it. Jamie flicked through the sheaf of pictures, evidence of the number of people who went into the clinic in the last months. How many of them were still able to function? How many more were dead?

Then she saw another face she knew. The image was grainy, but the features of the men were clearly visible from the street lights. The bald man she had seen with Cameron and a heavy-set bodyguard helped, or perhaps dragged, Blake into the side door of the clinic building. Blake's face was blank, as if he didn't see what was around him, his vacant expression that of a junkie in another realm. Jamie felt her heart wrench at his face, a little boy lost in the labyrinth of his mind. Someone with his kind of psychic ability would be invaluable to intelligence research. Had RAIN been targeting him since the beginning? Or was Blake suffering some kind of breakdown at the death of his father?

The photo was date stamped two nights ago. The fact that Blake hadn't contacted her meant he was either very sick or held without his consent. Jamie thought of the last entry in Lyssa's diary, the abuse she had suffered, the darkness in her mind that RAIN had amplified. She needed to get Blake out of there, but her partner needed her. Jamie called Missing-hall again, the phone ringing until it switched to voicemail.

"Pick up, pick up," she whispered, her mind filled with visions of what could be happening. She knew she had to make a choice.

CHAPTER 26

As Missinghall finished the delicious glass of wine, the Members started to move out of the Churchill Room and into the corridor on their way to the House of Commons Chamber for the debate. He stood to one side to let them all pass, shaking his head a little. He was suddenly unclear as to why he was here, anyway. There was a shiny edge to his vision, and like a filter on a lens, it intensified the light around him.

There was a buzzing in his pocket, but he couldn't take a phone call right now. His head was fuzzy, spinning far more than a glass of wine should make it. Whatever it was didn't matter anyway because the Houses of Parliament were stunning and he was captivated by the beauty around him. The dappled light from the windows patterned the great tapestries on the walls and made them come alive with golden rays. Sea battles raged with majestic ships that danced upon the blue ocean waves. He could almost taste the salt spray in the air and hear the cry of the sailors as they climbed the rigging, the words of *Rule Britannia* echoing in his mind. Missinghall smiled, a broad grin that transformed his face as he gazed into the tableau before him.

Then a dark cloud passed across the sun, and the light from the stained glass cast a red glow across the room. Missinghall frowned as the waves in the tapestry began to undulate faster, their violence shaking the ships in their midst. Shadows under the waters blackened into the shapes of sea monsters, giant squid with flailing limbs tipped with razor-sharp talons. One long tentacle arched out of the water, wrapping itself around a sailor and dragging him into the water. His screams echoed through the hall and Missinghall watched in horror as the man was sliced in two, body parts floating on the waves as blood turned the sea crimson around him. A flash of silver-grey. The sharks arrived, powering through the water, teeth ripping to shreds what the monsters dragged into the churning water.

Lightning ripped through the tapestry, as storm clouds gathered above the boats, like vengeful gods punishing mankind for the hubris of happiness. Wind whipped around the boats, spinning them in the vortex of waves, casting men into the depths of the sea, at the mercy of the creatures waiting beneath. The waves churned with blood, whipped into foam by the feeding frenzy of the sharks. The purple of the angry sky bled into black at the horizon, a promise of the ultimate end. Missinghall fell to his knees, tears on his cheeks as he witnessed the destruction, desperate to save the men before him. He clutched at the tapestry, screaming into the storm.

"Sir, please. It's OK, sir," a voice came in his ear, as strong arms pulled Missinghall away. "There's nothing there. You're having some kind of attack."

"No," he roared, pushing back violently against them, his eyes fixed on the horror before him. "I have to help. Let me be."

The next moment, Missinghall was down on the ground, two large security guards pinning him down. His head spun with the sound of the ocean storm, the screams of the dying, and the words of caution spoken in his ear were just a whisper. He closed his eyes to shut out the horror and succumbed to the pull of the deep.

***

Entering the Chamber of the House of Commons, Matthew Osborne clutched his notes, looking up at the statues on either side of the arched wall. They portrayed Winston Churchill and David Lloyd George, Prime Ministers during the war years, both with one foot polished to a shine where Members had touched them for luck on the way in. He took a deep breath, experiencing a rush of pride at how far he had come, although he knew that this was likely the final time he would stand here. Behind him, Matthew heard a shout from the direction of the Churchill Room, quickly stilled into silence. Whatever it was, there was no way to stop this now. He hurried inside.

The Gothic design was stark in comparison to the Lords' Chamber, but there were touches of ornate decoration in the wood paneling towards the public balcony above. The adversarial layout, green benches facing each other, was due to the original use as St Stephen's Chapel. But there was no reverent hush here anymore, much to the appalled spectators' surprise, as Parliament was full of shouting and noise, refereed by the Speaker of the House.

Matthew watched the other Members move to their usual places in the Chamber, chatting to other MPs, alert for gossip that might be used against people once considered friends. He had played this game for years now and still didn't have the power to change things. Yet it moved him to be part of the legacy this room handed down across the years. Despite the inevitable human failings of the Ministers in the House of Commons and the House of Lords, most of what they enacted was for the good of the nation. Matthew still believed in democratic government, but sometimes a more dramatic statement was needed to bring attention to a cause.

He looked at his watch and then up at the gallery where

the TV cameras and journalists stood, pads in hand. The drug was reasonably fast acting, quicker on some than others, but he was counting on being able to at least start the discussion on the Bill before its effects were felt. The Speaker of the House sat down and Matthew stepped to the front bench as the murmur of the crowd subsided.

"Honorable Members. Mr Speaker. Today is the Second Reading of the Mental Health Amendment Bill and I will start by outlining the abuses of the government agency, RAIN, the Research into Advanced Intelligence Network."

Matthew began to read from his prepared speech, and it seemed as if his consciousness split in two. He functioned on autopilot as an experienced public speaker, well used to performing in this venue. He was confident that the text of his speech would be analyzed later, and the scope of RAIN would finally be exposed. Another part of him focused on watching the faces of the Members who had been in the drinks reception.

The Prime Minister adjusted his tie and opened his collar a little. The honorable Member for Windsor was beginning to sweat, patches spreading in semicircles under his arms as he dabbed at his brow with a handkerchief. The cabal of Ministers from the North looked a little confused as they glanced around the room, eyes narrowing with suspicion at the opposition. Meanwhile, the press in the gallery looked bored, junior reporters on the graveyard political shift, hoping desperately for some kind of interesting news.

Matthew moved into the contentious part of his speech, calling for greater rights for the mentally ill. The insults began to fly, the cacophony of shouting in the room growing louder as he let the sound buoy him up, allowing it to rise without trying to respond. He wanted the temperature in the room to soar. He imagined molecules of the drug bonding with neurons in the brains around him, beginning to alter their consciousness, taking their emotions to extremes, numbing their prefrontal cortex and removing their self-control. The way the establishment had stolen control from Lyssa.

***

Harriet Arbuthnot felt the prickle of sweat under her arms and her head began to swim as she listened to the drone of that idiot, Matthew Osborne. Must have had a little too much wine, she thought, refocusing on the speaker. He was such a pompous ass, like most of the Members, but of course she mildly flirted with him as she did with others. She looked at his face more closely. It was shining, his eyes a brilliant blue and his mouth appeared to speak in slow motion, like his words came from under a swimming pool, distorted and slow.

It was so hot in here. Harriet looked up at the windows at the top of the gallery and felt the radiance of the sun like a furnace on her skin. *Why couldn't they sort out the air conditioning in here?* she wondered. Her eyes drifted down to the green back-benches opposite, her usual form of meditation. But instead of the calm vertical stripes, the emerald lines began to move in rippling swells. A wave of nausea rose up within her and Harriet put a hand to her mouth, eyes wide as she stared. The benches morphed into thick snakes, their heads rising up from the wooden paneling, tongues flickering in the air. She closed her eyes for a moment, shaking her head a little, part of her understanding that she must somehow be sick. She opened her eyes again and let out a scream as the bench around her twisted into a nest of serpents. Harriet leapt to her feet.

"Help me," she cried, clutching onto the seat behind her, trying to clamber away from the snakes. She could hear the clicking of the cameras from the gallery above, but the MPs around her just stared. Harriet was shocked at the hate in their faces, their mouths twisted in grimaces and their eyes blazing with murderous rage as shouting erupted in the Chamber. She felt the slithering of thick bodies around her legs and whimpered as the snakes wound around her body, pinning her to the bench with a heavy weight as she stared down at the melee before her.

One of the Members launched himself across the room towards Osborne, fists raised as he screamed abuse. The press clamored on the balcony as they tried to get the best footage. The action seemed to disintegrate any reserve left in the room, as the two sides of the Chamber rose to their feet. Men from either sides clambered down to the middle of the room and the thump of fists against flesh could soon be heard above the din. Harriet watched the thick green snakes writhe in and out of the bodies, fangs glistening, coils wrapped around the figures below. She was crying now, desperate for this to end but pinioned to the bench and unable to move. Her heart pounded in her chest and the sound of her own pulse thudded in her head as the shouting in the room grew louder. It was overlaid by another voice, whispering spite and hate, insidious with vile suggestion that spurred the mania to a new dimension.

A scream rang out and Harriet saw two of the Members holding down Miriam Lender, MP for Banbury. She could only watch as Miriam struggled against them. Another man tugged away her skirt and a serpent slithered across Miriam's bare belly as the man between her legs began to unbuckle his pants. Harriet's screams were frozen in her throat, tears running down her cheeks as she bore witness to the frenzy around her. One of the MPs drove another man's head against the wooden end of the bench, bashing it until blood ran onto the floor. Two others kicked a third, who lay prone on the stairs, hands wrapped around his head.

Security guards ran into the Chamber, blowing whistles and dragging some of the Members off each other. But there were too few of them and the brawling men turned on the security guards, pulling them down and kicking at their heads. Harriet watched as some of the Members tried to escape, but there were so few exits in the Chamber and bodies of others blocked their path. She couldn't tear her eyes away from the maelstrom below as it disintegrated into a writhing mass of confusion.

Suddenly, someone grabbed her from behind, an arm around her neck, pulling her over the back of the bench. Harriet struggled, squirming to escape the grip but the man pulled harder, grunting with exertion. Her vision began to fade as the lack of oxygen left her gasping.

"Stay still, you bitch," the man rasped. She felt two more sets of arms and then someone lifted her feet up, helping the men to pull her over the bench. The thick green snake wound around her body tightened its grip. She couldn't breathe, couldn't see properly, but she felt their hands on her and she stared up at the ceiling, her brain screaming, her mouth frozen in silence as darkness descended.

***

As the hallucinogens kicked in and the Chamber erupted into violence, Matthew looked around for the Prime Minister, the man whose signature supporting RAIN had damned his sister, the man who justified abuse of power with no regard for the lives destroyed in the process. Glen Abrahams rolled on the floor with his Lord Chancellor, the animosity between the men finally spilling over into thrown punches and attempted strangulation. Matthew couldn't help but grin at how this would look on the evening news, the likely resignation of the man he despised, the madness of these ineffectual politicians who would have spurned his Bill today. These few minutes would have dramatic consequences indeed.

A clumsy punch slammed into his back. Matthew spun round to see the Minister from Coventry North East, eyes wide and bloodshot, locked on visions beyond the physical realm. Matthew ducked easily under the man's second punch and slipped to the floor. He needed to get out. The police would be here soon, and he didn't have to stay any longer to know his plan was complete.

Matthew dropped to the floor, and crawled around the edge of the brawling crowd. Outside in the corridor, he saw uniformed police and more security guards rushing to the scene. He stepped back to let them past, the noise from the Chamber echoing around the grand entrance hall as he left the building just before the shut-down siren sounded.

CHAPTER 27

JAMIE FOLDED THE PHOTOGRAPH of Blake into her jacket pocket and with gloved hands placed the rest of the images on Matthew Osborne's desk. This whole place would need to be processed later, but it might be too late for Blake by then. She had to get him out of RAIN, but first, her responsibility was to her partner. She turned and ran down the stairs.

***

Pulling up in front of the Houses of Parliament ten minutes later, Jamie parked the bike in the Sovereign's Entrance just as the rain started to hammer down. Pedestrians hurried past to the shelter of the underground, umbrellas raised as they splashed through puddles. As Jamie tugged her helmet off, she heard an alarm ringing throughout the building. Something had already happened. *Please let him be OK*, she thought, desperate to get to Missinghall. She had sent him here, she had put him in harm's way.

The siren wail of ambulances and police cars scythed through the rain and cars parted on the road to let them through. People stopped on the pavement to watch, the atmosphere of high drama in the air. Jamie pushed through the gathering crowd and ran to the entrance hall, where a line of tourists was being held at the security gates. She showed her warrant card to one of the uniformed police.

"I need to get in there," Jamie said. "My partner's inside, along with a murder suspect. Please let me through."

The officer bent to look more closely at her card. "Sorry, Detective. We're under shut-down protocol, and so's every government building in the city. No one's coming in here now." He shook his head. "It's chaos in there anyway, and it looks like the bastard who did this got out before we closed everything down."

Shouting burst from the corridor behind the security area and a flurry of activity turned heads. An ambulance crew wheeled out gurneys with unconscious figures slumped upon them. Jamie's heart thumped in her chest, desperately hoping Missinghall wasn't among them.

"Clear the area! Let them through."

The uniformed officers onsite pushed the tourists aside to allow the medical staff by. Jamie looked down at the faces of the victims as they passed, some recognizable from the media, all high profile. Jamie realized that St Paul's had only ever been a practice run – this was Matthew Osborne's endgame.

A gurney came past with a big man lying prone, hands manacled to the side. His head was bruised and he wasn't moving.

"No," Jamie whispered, her hand flying to her mouth. She stepped out to the ambulance crew, holding her warrant card high.

"Please," she said. "That's my partner, he's a policeman. Detective Constable Alan Missinghall. Is he going to be alright?"

One of the medics waved at her. "Get clear," he said. "We have to get this lot to the hospital."

Jamie stepped back, allowing them through. She clenched

her fists, turning to push through the crowd back to her bike. The rain was heavier now but she held her face up to it, letting it soak her dark hair. Where would Matthew Osborne go? He must know that all officers would be out looking for him, so he wouldn't return to his flat. She thought back to their first conversation, when she had realized the depth of his love for his sister. Had he said anything that would help her find him? She closed her eyes and let the rain trickle down her face and into her leather jacket as she replayed the interview in her mind.

There was one place he had mentioned. The Tower of London, and how Lyssa had seen it as a metaphor for her mind, locked down to protect the treasures within. Anything was worth a try at this point, and Jamie needed to reach Matthew before anyone else. She understood his grief and maybe, just maybe, she could convince him to give himself up. She owed Missinghall that. Jamie kicked the bike into life and roared off down Victoria Embankment.

Urgency fueled Jamie's ride as she swerved the bike through traffic along the north bank of the Thames. Darkness had fallen now and the rain made visibility difficult. She pulled off the main road into Lower Thames Street, ignoring the signage to ride along the pedestrianized area down to the walkway on the riverside. Then she saw Tower Bridge, the two halves splitting open, starting to rise up into the air to allow ships through underneath. Osborne had said that sometimes he would watch it with Lyssa. Jamie revved the bike onwards.

***

Matthew felt the vibrations of the bridge as it started to part, the two halves slowly swinging upwards on their scheduled opening. He sat for a moment absorbing the physical pulse of the structure, wedged into an access doorway at the base of the north tower. He had slipped inside as security guards had cleared the bridge, the routine operation nothing special to them. He heard voices approach and fade again and then only the sounds of machinery reverberated through the structure. It was time.

He clutched the gun in his pocket, the unusual weight of it making him feel unbalanced. He had bought the Glock 17 a few weeks ago, when he had made the decision to avenge Lyssa and punish those who had exploited her. In the end, a gun wasn't right for them, but it was a good option for what he had planned tonight.

Cracking the door a little, Matthew could see the barriers closed in the distance and the bridge all but empty. The angle of the slope was getting steeper as one half rose into the air in front of him. He needed to get as high as he could, and he wanted one last glimpse of this city of grand beauty. He took a deep breath and started to walk briskly up the ever-steepening incline, every second a chance to be alone up there.

"Matthew!" A shout came from the crowd. "Stop!"

Matthew turned, seeing a black-clad figure with the security team. She was waving at him frantically. It was the police officer who had interviewed him after Monro's death. He started to run, panting now the incline was sharper, the bridge still rising inexorably.

There were more shouts behind him. Matthew looked back to see her break through the guards and come after him. *She can't catch me now*, he thought, pushing himself harder, chest bursting. Reaching the top, he hooked his arm around the railing at the side of the bridge as the incline steepened further. Matthew looked out at the Thames, winding through the city he loved, and smiled. It was so beautiful.

"Matthew," a voice came from below. "Please wait."

He looked down to see Detective Jamie Brooke, now almost below him as the bridge rose to vertical and they both clung to the side. She climbed towards him, her hazel eyes almost amber in the lights, burning with a righteous anger.

"Stop there, Detective. Don't come any further."

Jamie paused below, but her body was tense, ready to move quickly.

"I need to know," she called up. "The drug you put in the wine – will they recover from it? My friend was in there. He's a police officer, a good man with a family. He shouldn't have been there."

"I'm sorry about your friend," Matthew said. "But there's always collateral damage, and RAIN never cared for the lives they ruined." His voice softened, and he smiled gently, shaking his head. "But I'm not like them, Detective, and the effects of the drug are temporary. Your friend will be fine in a few days, as will those bastards who deserved it. I just hoped to give them some perspective, some empathy – but I won't be here to see it." Matthew looked out across the water to the battlements lit up before them, a bastion of the British monarchy for almost a thousand years. "I've always found the Tower to be an inspiration. From the outside it's symbolic of strength, but it's really like our minds, full of rooms where nightmares and violence lie hidden. Where skeletons are buried, and evil deeds are committed in the dark. Tell me, Detective, have you stood at the place where Anne Boleyn was beheaded? There's a resonance you can feel, a mental scream that echoes through the centuries. That scream continues in the way we deal with the mad, in the way Lyssa was treated, in the way that RAIN deals with those who are different."

"RAIN will be investigated," Jamie said. "Your speech is all over the news, so you've made sure they will be held accountable."

Matthew shook his head. "I have my doubts about that, but I can't do any more. Hating means that you're still alive, but I have no hate left now. I've done what I can, but RAIN is bigger than all of us. You don't know how powerful they are. They take anyone they want and if they're not mad already, they become so in their care. They could take you, Detective, and if I'm still around tomorrow, for sure they'll take me in recompense for my actions. Those who are sectioned have no choice."

Matthew began to climb over the railings, pulling himself up, the veins in his arms bulging at the physical effort required to lift his own weight over the edge.

"Don't do it, Matthew," Jamie whispered, reaching towards him. "Lyssa would have wanted you to stay, continue your work. You said you wanted to help others."

He turned his head to look at her, eyes clear and focused. "I know this is my end, and I go happily. But what of your grief, Detective? Perhaps you want to join me. A second's jump into blackness is nothing, a moment of panic perhaps and then oblivion. Is your life as worthless as mine is without Lyssa, I wonder?" Matthew reached out a hand. "Jump with me. End your own suffering."

CHAPTER 28

Jamie looked at Matthew's outstretched hand and thought of Polly's ashes on the shelf in her cold, dark flat. Part of her wanted to take this chance and step with him into blackness. Together, it would be easy, but perhaps it was the hard things that were the most worthwhile in life. She thought of Blake, held in the RAIN clinic, under the authority of the man she'd seen in Scotland Yard with Dale Cameron. She had to help him now.

"No," she said to Matthew. "I have someone who can help me live again. But I understand why you want this and I won't stand in your way. I won't make you suffer any more than you have already."

Jamie backed away and carefully began the descent to the road level of the bridge. She didn't look back, but all her senses were heightened in anticipation.

As she neared the bottom of the struts, she called on her radio.

"Suspect on Tower Bridge. Requesting backup."

A moment later, a shot rang out in the night air and Jamie turned to see Matthew's body fall from the apex of the bridge. The slip of the wind seemed to whisper 'Lyssa' as he fell, a caress as he went to meet his sister.

Jamie touched her radio again. "Suspect has jumped from

Tower Bridge. Gunshot heard, possible suicide. Requesting backup from Marine Police and a river search team."

The Marine Police boat arrived quickly, its searchlight sweeping the dark water for Matthew Osborne. It didn't take long before they dragged a body from the water slightly down-river. Jamie found herself holding her breath, wanting him to have found his escape. The police on deck pulled a body bag out and Jamie knew that Matthew was gone. She was grateful that fate had not been so cruel as to leave him here.

Jamie stood for a moment looking down into the river, the eddies in the current reflecting her indecision. The Detective Sergeant side of her knew she should return to the police station and report on everything, be a part of the Westminster case gathering the evidence. She pulled the photo of Blake from her inside jacket pocket, her fingertips trailing across his haunted face.

CHAPTER 29

THE ARCHWAYS OF LONDON Bridge were only a few blocks away. Jamie cruised the back streets of the area, her eyes scanning the passages underneath the branching railway tracks, fanning out from one of the biggest stations in the city. The sheer blue sides of the Shard towered over her, a symbol of wealth in this rejuvenated part of London. She pulled into one street, recognizing the looming structures of Guy's Hospital. The arches opposite looked familiar, so she ducked the bike down a side alley. Stopping to pull out the picture of Blake, Jamie could see that this was the place.

The clinic had a professional facade, with opaque glass over the front and discreet signage indicating it was a mental health practice. There were some lights on but no movement or shadows inside. The next two archways had no signage and only the last one had a door on it with just a keypad. Did the clinic stretch further inside the structure?

On a nearby corner, a twenty-four-hour greasy spoon cafe was still open, advertising all-day breakfast for a few pounds. It was the type of place that did so well next to a bastion of health, as people craved comfort food and sweet tea when faced with terrible news. Jamie parked the bike and headed into the cafe, ordering a mug of tea and sitting in the window, so she could watch the clinic.

As she sipped the tea, Jamie thought of Blake, lost in his nightmare visions and how she had done Cameron's bidding by involving him in the case. She was responsible for Blake being in there, so she needed to get him out. Lyssa Osborne had died because of what RAIN did to her in there, amplifying her internal anguish, making her believe there was no point in living. Jamie didn't want to lose Blake in the same way.

The progression of night changed the types of people walking this area from professionals scurrying home late from the office, to those seeking oblivion from the day's stress. There were nightclubs under some of the arches, their doorways hidden by graffiti elevated to the level of street art through vivid detail and color. The clubs drew seekers and Jamie wondered whether the clinic found some of its clients from those who had lost the path completely.

This area of Southwark, south of the river, had been the red-light district, the entertainment area for much of London's history. The Rose Theatre of Marlowe and Shakespeare's Globe had once stood here, the reconstruction of the Globe just minutes from where she sat. The pilgrims from Chaucer's *Canterbury Tales* met in the Tabard, a pub on the thoroughfare on the route to Canterbury near here. Just a street away, there was an unconsecrated graveyard known as Cross Bones for the outcast dead, the prostitutes and their children. The paupers had been forgotten in their own time, but now the place bloomed with flowers, left there by those seeking the favor of the dark shades.

There were a number of nurses walking home as the shift ended at Guy's, and several passed the window of the cafe, some laughing together, some with faces fixed in anxiety edged with desperation. Jamie knew that look from years of dealing with the public, of trying to serve those in need and being abused verbally every day and physically far too often.

One woman in a nurse's uniform caught her eye, as instead of walking past the cafe, she turned towards the door of the clinic.

Jamie ran out the door and across the road, reaching the clinic as the door shut behind the nurse. Jamie banged on it, hoping that the woman would think she had dropped something.

The door opened a crack. Jamie showed her police warrant card.

"Good evening, I need to speak to whoever is in charge. We have reason to believe you have a murder suspect here."

The nurse looked suspicious, her eyes narrowing to examine the card.

"We're not open, Detective …"

"Brooke," Jamie finished for her. "That doesn't matter. I need to speak with your night supervisor immediately."

At the authority in her tone, the nurse opened the door a little more.

"OK, but you'll need to wait here while I get him."

She pulled open the door and Jamie stepped into a waiting area, just like any up-market clinic, with piles of magazines and even a bowl of sweets on the countertop. The nurse indicated a chair.

"Please wait here. I won't be long."

Jamie picked up a magazine and looked away slightly, turning back to watch as the nurse entered a number on a keypad by the door and stepped through as it buzzed. Four, six, five, two, nine. Jamie repeated the numbers in her mind and before the door shut, she moved swiftly to stop it closing. As she listened to the woman's footsteps clacking down the hallway, Jamie's heart thudded in her chest. She couldn't wait for whoever was in charge to check on her warrant card, especially if, as she suspected, Dale Cameron was involved in Blake's admission.

She heard the nurse go through another door and Jamie

slipped into the corridor behind her, closing the outer door firmly. There were several more doors off to the side but for now, Jamie just needed to hide. There was no time to find Blake now, so she needed to wait until they thought she was gone.

Jamie tried a few doors. The first was an interview room, just a table and some chairs with nowhere to hide. The second was dark, so Jamie pulled out her tiny flashlight. It was an office suite with computers and a bank of old-fashioned filing shelves on one side, with winding handles to make more space. She ducked inside, pushing the door quietly closed, and wound the shelves partly open, squashing herself down the back, away from the view of the door. Seconds later, she heard voices in the corridor.

The angry, low tones of a man interrupted the voice of the nurse, but Jamie couldn't hear what they were saying. She hoped they wouldn't check for her, assuming she had left the building out of the main door. After they had gone back into the front office, she heard raised voices in a discussion and then they faded away down the corridor again.

Jamie waited, concentrating on her breathing for ten minutes, twenty, then half an hour. How long would it be until they had forgotten her and just continued with the routine of the night? She looked around at the files on the shelves, realizing they were medical records, inpatient folders and test results. Jamie pulled one off the shelf near her, holding the tiny flashlight in her teeth to read. There was little to indicate anything wrong here, but the sheer volume of records was overwhelming.

She looked at her watch. It was nearly two a.m., and the adrenalin of the day was wearing off. She was tired, which meant that the people on duty must be, as well. She couldn't go in with guns blazing, she didn't even have a weapon, but she had to try and find Blake. She stood, stretching her limbs.

Pulling open the office door a little, Jamie listened, but all was silent and the corridor was dark. Her tiny flashlight illuminated the hallway, so she advanced slowly, trying more doors along the way. There was another office, then an examination room with nothing untoward in it. It looked like an outpatient clinic, perhaps somewhere to screen those that RAIN might be interested in. The door at the end of the corridor looked more hopeful, but it had a keypad on it.

Jamie tried the numbers she had seen the nurse use. Four, six, five, two, nine. The door buzzed and she pushed it open slowly, expecting to see one of the staff but once again, there was just a corridor with doors leading off it. By the angle, it stretched far into the building next door. Jamie stood listening quietly for a moment. There was a faint beep of medical equipment coming from the rooms around her, but no sound of movement. She kept trying doors, until she came to one set up like a hospital ward. Jamie held her breath, not daring to move, her heart pounding as she realized there were bodies in the beds, chests rising and falling rhythmically.

Nobody moved, no alarms went off. Jamie swung her flashlight around the room. There were four beds, with a person in each, but all were hooked up to drips and seemed to be deeply unconscious. Was Blake one of them?

She quickly checked each one, all young men, but no Blake. Jamie frowned. It was strange that they would all be sedated, but perhaps it was a way to avoid extra staffing. There were no charts on the beds, but there was an empty nurses' station. Jamie bent to the desk and shuffled through the paperwork. The sheets for the four men were stamped with 'Transfer,' but beneath them was a procedural document on managing insulin coma. Jamie pulled it out, reading the words but not quite believing them. It seemed these men had been 'recruited' locally from the homeless population and were now being used as test subjects for a new form of insulin coma therapy. Popular in the 1930s, insulin was injected to decrease blood sugar causing the subjects to descend into seizures and eventually a soporific coma that could be revived through intravenous blood sugar with the aim of shocking the system into recovery. The notes on this document implied they were being given the treatment in combination with ECT, and they would be transferred to the long-term RAIN facility the next day. Jamie took out her smartphone and snapped a couple of pictures of the paper-work and the bodies of the men in the beds illuminated by torchlight.

She replaced the documents and edged out of the room into the corridor again. The next room was a similar ward, but this time with a curtain obscuring the back half. Jamie tiptoed closer, hearing the rhythmic breathing of a person behind the curtain. She peered around to see Blake's face on the pillow, his head closely shaved. Her heart leapt.

"Blake," she whispered. "I'm here. Wake up."

No response. Jamie stepped behind the curtain and leaned down to his ear. "Blake. Wake up." She touched his shoulder. Still no response.

His face was calm in repose but there were dark shadows under his eyes and even in the few days since she had seen him, he had become gaunt and thin. His arm was hooked to an IV and Jamie pulled the tubing from the cannula, hoping that the sedation would stop and he might come round. There was no way she could get him out while he was unconscious. She saw the shackles on his wrists and knew then that he hadn't come in willingly.

Jamie looked around the back half of the room, noting a chair with restraints and a head brace. What had they done to him? Jamie leaned down and stroked Blake's forehead, his skin dark against the white pillow. He moaned a little, his face twisting.

She had to get the cuffs off him. Jamie walked to the chair

and saw the trolley next to it, with medical instruments in a neat line. There was a key in the perfect line of implements, as if placed there by an OCD torturer. Picking it up, she unlocked Blake's cuffs, gently freeing his scarred hands. She tucked them into the sheets as she waited, hoping the drugs would wear off enough that he would wake soon. Meanwhile, she needed to find evidence of what this lab was for.

At the back of the room was a white workbench, with a closed laptop and paperwork filed neatly next to it. Jamie looked through the pile of papers, finding a thick brown file with Blake's name on the front and an old book, bound in burgundy leather. She opened the file to find a sheaf of photos, taken over a period of years by the looks of them. There were some images taken more recently, at the Imperial War Museum a few days ago and some of an older man, his face similar to Blake's. Putting the photos aside, she scanned the papers, finding two versions of a family tree – one handwritten on thin paper and the other a typed medicalized version, similar to the one she had seen at Monro's psychiatric practice. The two had some differences, but both were clearly of Blake's extended family. Jamie turned to look back at the bed, Blake's wan face on the pillow. RAIN clearly wanted to understand his genetic history, but how far would they go to get it?

Suddenly she heard a sound in the corridor, the squeak of wheels and the slow footsteps of someone approaching.

CHAPTER 30

JAMIE SLIPPED ROUND BLAKE'S bed, ducking down behind the curtain, folding herself out of sight of the door. She heard a rush of air as it opened and the steps of someone coming into the room. Her heart pounded in her chest, her pulse racing. They couldn't find her now, not when she was so close.

The wheels of the trolley squeaked closer. If it was a nurse with night meds, they would see very soon that the IV was unhooked. They would know she was here. She had to move. Jamie grasped the handle of her tiny flashlight, ready to use it as a weapon, and braced herself to jump forward.

"I know you're here, Detective." A smooth voice filled the room and Jamie started at the unexpected sound. "You might as well come out and we can talk. I know you're worried about your friend, but perhaps I can explain his treatment. This is a hospital, after all." The man sounded reasonable and Jamie stood, unfolding herself from the folds of the curtain.

It was the bald man she had seen with Cameron at the station, his head a strange asymmetrical shape. His dual-colored eyes were sharp and focused.

"Detective Brooke, my nurse said you were looking for me. I'm Dr Crowther, and I would have shown you the facility if you'd requested it. But now you're here, you can see that

Blake is fine. He's restrained for his own good – we had to stop him self-harming after the death of his father."

"I want to talk to him," Jamie said, keeping her eyes fixed on Crowther. "I want to know that he's consented to be here."

Crowther frowned.

"You know he's mentally ill, don't you? He supposedly sees visions of other dimensions, of the past. All evidence of insanity, which we can help him recover from. I can tell him you were here when he wakes up tomorrow, and we can arrange for you to visit at a more … sociable time of day." He gestured towards the door. "Let me escort you out."

Jamie hesitated. Crowther was being so reasonable, implying she could visit Blake easily tomorrow. She thought of the men down the hall locked into insulin comas with transfer papers. But perhaps Blake wouldn't even be here if she came back later.

Crowther's eyes narrowed as if he could see her hesitation and his hand slipped into his pocket. Seeing the movement, Jamie shoved the bed with her leg, smashing the metal frame into his knee, as he whipped something from his pocket and sprayed it directly in her face. Jamie felt the sting of pepper, her eyes streaming, and she began to cough, her lungs seizing up. She dropped to the floor, bending over and heaving as she tried to draw air into her lungs. Crowther's boot thudded into her side and she rolled sideways, pain exploding through her body, panic descending as she fought to breathe.

"You silly bitch," he sneered. "You think you can just walk in here and take my prize specimen away?" He kicked her again. Jamie gasped, fighting for air. "You have no idea who's involved in this. Your boss, Cameron, he knows, and you'll find you have no place in the police now. Not ever again." He reached down and grabbed Jamie's arm, dragging her up and into the chair. "Now, why don't we try and send you a little mad? I hear you're close to the edge already and the main facility is always happy to get fresh brains to play with. No one's going to miss you anymore."

The chair was hard against her back and as she rubbed her eyes, Jamie felt her other hand clicked into place, manacled to the arm of the chair with a metal cuff. His words resonated through a haze of pain. Perhaps he was right. Without Polly, without Blake, no one would miss her. Missinghall would try to find out something, but he was hospitalized for now. She would be left inside whatever hell Crowther wanted, a lab rat for the mind, an experimental subject with no identity, just a label they decided on. In the past, women had been sent to Bedlam for nothing more than questioning their husband's authority, and now she would be sent there for challenging the supremacy of those in control.

"Let me go, you bastard. Help!"

Jamie shouted, twisting against the man, throwing her head back to try and hit him with her skull, reaching round with her arm, her eyes still blinded by the pepper spray.

"There's no one to hear you. No one who cares, anyway." He laughed, his voice further away now. "We just need a little sedation, and then you won't be able to speak. You won't remember anything but the nightmares that emerge in your sleep, when you wake covered in sweat, fear dripping from your pores." He fought with her, his higher position and strength giving him just enough leverage to click the manacle onto her other wrist. "You think you've seen the depths of what humans can do in your work, Detective, but what I show you in here, strapped to this chair, will send you right over the edge."

Jamie's eyes were clearing now, tears streaming down her face as they washed out the pepper spray. She could see the hazy outline of Blake in the bed. Crowther filled a syringe with green liquid, a smile of triumph on his face. She twisted her body, shaking her arms, pulling at the restraints, desperate to get away. Once she was drugged, she would be out of control, and she would truly be whatever he wanted her to be.

He turned with the syringe in his hand.

"Now, if you hold still, this will be more pleasant for both of us. Or, I can restrain you even further. Regardless, you will be sedated. This particular concoction also has amnesiac side effects."

Behind the doctor, Jamie saw Blake move his head towards the sound. His eyelids were fluttering. She tried not to look at him, willing him to wake up fully.

"Surely it would be more fun for you to torture me without sedation," she said, trying to keep Crowther's eyes on her. Behind him, Blake opened his eyes.

The doctor smiled. "Who said anything about torture? This is research, Detective, a scientific endeavor that gives this country a competitive advantage. Think about it. If we can find ways to turn off empathy and regret, our soldiers will be more effective in the field. If we can find a way to kill sexuality in the brain, we will no longer have sex offenders. If we can find a way to make people commit suicide, we will rid the world of those hangers on, the drain on society that means we all pay so much in benefits. If we can control behavior and emotion, then we will truly be the most powerful country on Earth. To learn all this, to test all this, we need subjects. You should consider your participation to be the ultimate in service to your country. You would have joined the police for similar reasons, surely, Detective?"

Crowther took another step towards Jamie, syringe held ready. Behind him, Blake was slowly sitting up, realizing his limbs were unshackled.

"I chose the police in order to make a difference," Jamie said. "But my actions within the force were my own choice. The people you experiment on come to you for care, and you abuse their trust by treating them as test subjects. Your research would be banned if the public ever knew of it."

"The public?" Crowther snorted. "They couldn't give a shit about the mentally ill. They just want to be protected, defended and made well again. Those half-assed liberals still want the best for themselves and their own children, and our research will give them that future." He took another step forward. "And your sacrifice will help."

CHAPTER 31

Blake reached for his IV stand. As he did, he brushed the metal cuff on the side of the bed. Crowther turned at the clanging sound and dropped the needle in his haste to reach the panic button on the side wall. As he moved, Jamie kicked out, knocking him down. Crowther scrambled to his feet but Blake was up now, swinging the heavy IV stand down to smash onto the doctor's back. He moaned, but still crawled forward.

"Hit him again," Jamie shouted. They couldn't let him press that panic button.

Blake shifted his grip, his face set in a grimace. He slammed the IV stand down again, the metal bottom smashing into the side of Crowther's head. The doctor slumped to the floor, unconscious. Blake stared down at him, his eyes still vague and hazy.

"He won't be out for long," Jamie said. "Blake, look at me. You need to get me out of these shackles. We both need to get out of here."

Blake looked up, his face twisting with anguish. "I don't know what's real anymore. What I see and what he made me see. Am I really crazy, Jamie?"

"Come here," Jamie whispered, longing to hold him. "Just breathe and listen to my heartbeat." He walked forward and laid his head on her stomach. She wanted to stroke his head, like she used to do for Polly, but her hands were still shackled. "That's what's real. I'm real. You're real. And we need to get out of here."

After a moment, Blake stood up straight again, his eyes clearing of clouds, the blue sharpening as some of the natural color returned to his face.

"You're strapped down," he said.

Jamie smiled. "Good to see you're paying attention. The keys are over there, I think." She indicated with a nod of her head to where a number of implements lay next to the doctor's laptop. Blake found the key and unlocked her cuffs, his movements unsteady.

Jamie rubbed her wrists and then swung her legs off the chair, adrenalin fading as tiredness washed over her. "We have to get out of here, right now." Blake leaned against the chair, clutching at it for support. "Can you walk?"

He nodded, his eyes determined. "I'll manage."

She grabbed the file with Blake's notes from the sideboard, shoving it in a large specimen bag. She added the syringe of green fluid, putting a plastic cap on to shield the needle. It was evidence of something, even if she didn't know quite what.

"That burgundy leather book as well," Blake said, his voice almost breaking. "It was my father's."

Jamie pushed the book inside the bag, then turned to help Blake towards the door. There was a doctor's coat hanging there. As Blake pulled it on to hide his patient's gown, he sighed heavily.

"Are you sure I'm not meant to be in here, Jamie?" He looked unsure. "I saw things when my father died, things that made me wonder whether something is wrong in my head. And my visions here …" He shook his head. "I just don't know what to think."

Jamie squeezed his hand. "If there's something wrong,

we'll find it out together. We'll get help on your terms. People come in here and disappear into the system. Some of them die, whether by their own hand or helped along by RAIN. I won't have that happen to you."

Her voice betrayed her emotion. For a moment, Jamie thought Blake would kiss her and she longed to feel his lips on hers. Just a moment of connection. But his eyes shadowed again and he nodded.

"Thank you. Let's go."

Jamie slowly opened the door of the room, listening for any other noise, but it was all quiet. They shuffled out together into the dark corridor. Blake leaned heavily on her shoulder, his breathing labored as they walked. Jamie relished the warmth of his body next to hers, her arm wrapped around his waist. She could feel the muscles under his skin, realizing it was the first time she had really touched him. Their steps were slow but it wasn't far to the main exit. Just a few more minutes.

Red flashing lights suddenly illuminated the corridor in a silent alarm. A door slammed, and a roar of frustration echoed down the hallway.

"We have to run now," Jamie said, tightening her grip on Blake. "Crowther must have made it to the panic button."

Blake picked up his pace, but his legs were weak and he stumbled. His weight was too much for Jamie and he fell to his knees, coughing. His face was pale and haggard, the after-effect of the drugs pulling him back towards oblivion.

"You ... go on," he wheezed. "Leave me."

"After all this?" Jamie said. "I don't think so."

As she began to help Blake up, Crowther charged around the corner. Blood ran down his face from the wound on his head, and his eyes blazed fury. In the flashing red lights, he was a staccato nightmare. He threw himself at Jamie, knocking her to the floor, his weight pinning her to the ground. Blake slammed against the wall, knocked off his feet. The specimen bag fell open, its content skidding across the floor.

"Bitch," the doctor bellowed, drawing his arm back to smash into Jamie's face. Her police training was automatic and she bucked her hips hard, throwing him off balance as she turned sideways, raising her elbow. She slammed it into him, screaming her effort as she struck him in the side of his head.

Using the momentum, Jamie rolled fast, pushing Crowther away from her. Blake grabbed the doctor's neck in a headlock from behind, grimacing as he used every last ounce of energy to hold the man. Crowther fought, his fingers scrabbling at Blake's arms. In the flickering red lights, Jamie saw the rage in Blake's eyes, his intention to repay the torture he had undergone. Next to him, she caught sight of the syringe.

Grabbing it, she pulled the cap off and sat on Crowther's chest, pinning his arms down with her knees, while Blake yanked the doctor's head back, exposing his skin. Jamie thrust the needle against the doctor's neck, watching it pierce his flesh. She pressed down the plunger and he groaned, eyes fluttering in horror. Crowther struggled for a few more seconds and then went limp. The sound of panting breath filled the corridor as the red light still blinked its silent warning. Jamie met Blake's eyes and saw her own exhaustion mirrored there.

"Now, we really have to get out of here," she said. "He said that drug had amnesiac properties, so perhaps he won't even remember what happened here."

"I wanted to kill him," Blake said, his voice dull, as he looked at the unconscious body.

Jamie helped him up. "I know, but we can't leave a dead body here, and I don't think they'll come after us now. This is an organization that lives in the shadows."

She filled the specimen bag again, taking the empty syringe along with the book and papers. They left a lot of evidence behind, and RAIN could easily find her and Blake again, but somehow, she thought that they might find easier targets after this encounter. Her own involvement in the Matthew Osborne case was high profile enough, and if she was called to give evidence in court – well, she knew enough to worry the higher echelons of the organization.

Together, they hobbled down the corridor and out into the street, emerging between the arches of London Bridge station. The sky was bright with shades of pink and orange, heralding the dawn across the city. It was quiet and peaceful, as if nothing could possibly have happened here. These doorways held dark secrets but within hours, this area would be teeming with people working normal jobs, oblivious to what lay beneath.

"It's not far to my place," Jamie whispered. "You need to rest."

Blake nodded, his eyelids drooping as she helped him on the bike as a pillion passenger. His arms tight around her waist, she drove through the streets back to Lambeth. The events of the last days whirred through her mind, and she knew there was one more thing she had to do.

CHAPTER 32

LEAVING BLAKE IN HER bed, passed out from exhaustion, Jamie roared back towards New Scotland Yard on her bike. She registered the heaviness in her limbs as the adrenalin of the last few hours subsided. There was an anticlimax after action but the highs and lows were what drove her back to work. A mundane office job would never suit her; she needed this edge.

***

As she walked into the station towards her desk, a voice stopped her.

"Detective Sergeant Brooke. My office, please." Dale Cameron's voice had an edge of steel. He rarely called people by their full rank unless a dressing-down was on the way.

"Yes, sir." Jamie changed direction and went into his office, her heart thudding.

Cameron slammed the door shut.

"The Prime Minister and a load of MPs are in hospital, Missinghall's in there too, and you let Osborne jump," he barked. "Why?"

"I ... he ... I couldn't reach him," Jamie stuttered. Of course no one would understand the grief she had shared with Matthew, but who wouldn't let someone in that much agony find relief?

"You were captured on police helicopter cameras, and the video phones of spectators below. You know how powerful citizen journalism is nowadays and you're clearly shown leaving him to shoot himself as he jumped. There's evidence at his flat but his arrest and confession were paramount." Cameron paused and walked around his desk to sit in his chair. "Jamie, it's been a rough few months for you, but you've repeatedly flouted regulations. You've sent your partner into danger. God knows where you've been overnight when you should have been here working the case." Cameron rubbed his forehead, and exhaled slowly. "You're just not a team player, and I can't trust you anymore."

Jamie heard his words and it was like witnessing a slow-motion car crash. She could see what was coming, but she couldn't stop it. "I have no choice but to suspend you pending investigation. You're relieved of duty effective immediately."

Cameron's blue eyes glittered with triumph. By discrediting her and removing her from the task force, Jamie knew she would have no strong position to question his allegiance to RAIN or to make sure the organization was investigated in detail. Perhaps Cameron had been waiting for this opportunity since the Lyceum and the Hellfire Caves, the night she thought she had seen him in the murderous crowd.

"If you don't make too much of a fuss about this, I'll see you're just demoted and there'll be a decent position outside London. Perhaps it's time for a change, anyway. It might do you some good."

Jamie's heart thumped against her ribs as she repressed all the things she wanted to say to the bastard. Men like Cameron would always emerge unscathed from trouble and in this male-dominated hierarchy, his kind would always win. But the thought of leaving London disturbed her, for this was her home and memories of Polly lay across the city like an emotional map. She could trace their journey together in the tides of the Thames. Jamie took a deep breath, fighting back her angry words.

Finally, she nodded, unable to trust herself to speak, and turned towards the door.

"It's a shame, Jamie." Cameron shook his head. "I had high hopes for you."

She walked out and slammed the door shut behind her.

Jamie stood for a moment in the corridor, trying to hold back the tears that threatened, but she would not cry here, not where anyone could see her. Jamie thought of the day she had left her parents on the Milton Keynes housing estate, telling them she would be part of the Metropolitan Police, that she would be someone, she would make a difference. All she had ever wanted was to be remarkable and now, they were pushing her out. She had lost Polly, and now it seemed she would lose the job she loved as well.

Jamie closed her eyes for a moment, focusing on breathing, trying to remain calm. The rush of the last few days swirled about her. She saw Matthew Osborne's face before he jumped, Missinghall lying prone on a gurney, Blake unconscious in the hospital bed under the archways of London Bridge. She had a feeling that the investigation into RAIN would be stonewalled from higher up, perhaps the clinic was being emptied even now. Matthew Osborne's actions in Westminster were tainted by the murders he committed, and, as there could be no trial, he would soon be forgotten.

The hubbub of the police station surrounded her, sounds she had always associated with her place in the world. But suddenly Jamie knew it was time to move on. Her old life had died with Polly, and the police held too many memories. There were people she couldn't trust anymore, and Jamie knew she couldn't change it from the inside.

She turned and pushed into Cameron's office again. He looked momentarily surprised and then angry.

"I thought I told you ..."

"I resign," Jamie interrupted, her voice strong, with no hint of hesitation. She pulled her warrant card from her pocket and put it on Cameron's desk, her hazel eyes holding his. He broke the gaze first and she could see he understood what she knew. She spun on her heel and walked out of his office, down the corridor and into the day, a lightness in her step.

She steered the bike down to the Thames, parking near Tower Bridge where Matthew Osborne had ended his life. Jamie looked out over the fast-flowing water, feeling the breeze on her face as she gazed at the Tower of London on the north bank. Its strong walls had stood there while the inhabitants of London had gone about their mad lives for centuries, and it would continue to stand when she was gone.

This life was a puzzle and sometimes the pieces didn't fit, but the attempt was still worth it. Sometimes pieces were lost, as Polly was lost to her, but London was all about reinvention and rejuvenation, and tomorrow could be another life. She thought of Blake, asleep in her bed, and a smile flickered across her face. Jamie inhaled deeply, feeling more alive than she had for months.

ENJOYED DELIRIUM?

Thanks for joining Jamie and Blake in *Delirium*. Their adventures continue in *Deviance*. If you enjoyed the book, a review would be much appreciated as it helps other readers discover the story.

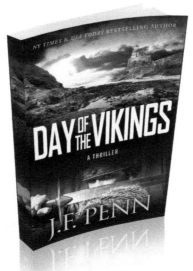

Get a free copy of the bestselling thriller, *Day of the Vikings*, an ARKANE thriller featuring Blake Daniel, when you sign up to join my Reader's Group. You'll also be notified of giveaways, new releases and receive personal updates from behind the scenes of my books.

Click here to get started:

www.JFPenn.com/free

AUTHOR'S NOTE

The themes of *Delirium* were born years ago when I studied psychology at the University of Auckland, New Zealand. I took classes in neuroscience and clinical psychology, as well as learning about issues of gender, individual differences and the history and abuses of psychiatry.

The motif on the title page and at the beginning of the chapters is a Rorschach ink blot, a psychological test where the individual interprets the image according to their own perception, used to diagnose underlying thought disorders. What do you see in the image?

You can see a collage of ideas for the book on Pinterest.com/jfpenn/delirium

History of mental illness

The Tranquilizer chair used as a method of murder in the Prologue is a real device. The person's head was encased in the padded box to block out light and sound, the legs and arms were pinioned and then hot and cold water applied to the head and feet. The other treatments mentioned are also historically accurate, although the story is, of course, fictionalized.

Bedlam, as Bethlem Hospital was known, moved to different locations over time. It was once at the site of the Imperial War Museum as described and is now in Beckenham,

South East London. I visited the museum at the current hospital, and it's a lovely, leafy campus with an art gallery as well as a cafe for visitors. The *Labyrinth* painting in the gallery scene is based on William Kurelek's *The Maze*, which I saw in the museum.

Three generations of the Monro family ran Bedlam, during which time it acquired its reputation as a kind of hell. For more, read *Undertaker of the Mind: John Monro and mad-doctoring in eighteenth-century England*, by Jonathan Andrews and Andrew Scull (2001). Bryan Crowther was a surgeon at Bedlam in the eighteenth century, rumored to have dissected the brains of dead inmates and to have donated their bodies to the resurrectionists, whose anatomy work I covered in *Desecration*.

I wanted to have a scene in Broadmoor because it's as well known in Britain as Bedlam once was. The men incarcerated there are extreme cases and in fact, very few people with mental health issues actually harm other people. They are far more likely to harm themselves, or commit suicide, than hurt others. You can learn more about Broadmoor through the NHS videos here: www.wlmht.nhs.uk/bm/broadmoor-hospital/about-broadmoor-hospital-video/

Research into Advanced Intelligence Network (RAIN) is based on the Intelligence Advanced Research Projects Agency (IARPA) www.iarpa.gov. This real American agency "invests in high-risk, high-payoff research programs that have the potential to provide the United States with an over-whelming intelligence advantage over future adversaries." I'm sure the British must have an equivalent!

Personal note

I have the utmost respect for people who are on the diag-nosed spectrum of mental illness, and for those who care for them, and so this book is more about the exploitation that has dominated the history of psychiatry. Whenever we consider people to be 'the Other,' there will always be abuse.

I also believe there is a spectrum of madness in all of us, it's just a matter of degree. We all have moments of craziness, inspired by life situations or through the influence of drugs, illegal or prescribed. Like many of us, I have caught glimpses of what some would call mental illness in my own life. I share these thoughts honestly, as a mentally well person living happily in society. I hope to demonstrate that the continuum is a slide we all move up and down, and perhaps help you reflect on where you sit. Here are some of my experiences:

If I drive at night, I want to steer into oncoming headlights. I have an almost overwhelming attraction, perhaps a compulsion, to smash into them. I have to tighten my hands on the steering wheel to stop my desire to turn into the path of death. For this reason, I don't drive at night unless I really have to.

When my first husband left me, my anger and grief caused me to want to self-harm. I wanted to hurt myself so badly that he would be driven back to me out of guilt. (That was years ago and I am now happily married again!)

I sometimes feel untethered from the world, as if my physical body is nothing and I could just leave it behind. I have moments of detachment where I don't care for anyone. I feel like an alien put on this planet and nothing matters. I look around and it could all disappear and I wouldn't care.

When I write, I sometimes read my words later and I can't remember writing it. I didn't even know I thought those things and I don't know how they arrived on the page.

I have experienced religious conversion, spoken in tongues and I once believed the world to be teeming with angels and demons. Perhaps I still do.

All these moments have passed over me in waves. They

are seconds in a life of nearly forty years as I write this, and UK statistics show that one in four people will experience some kind of mental health problem in the space of a year:

www.mentalhealth.org.uk/help-information/mental-health-statistics/

I'm not on any medication and I don't think I'm 'crazy,' whatever that means. I move up and down the spectrum and I expect to continue doing so during my allotted span.

My biggest fear in terms of mental health is to become demented and for my brain to die before my body does. Fantasy author Terry Pratchett's descent into early-onset Alzheimer's started my investigation into the choice to die. It is a writer's responsibility to think about the hard issues and suicide is certainly a contentious one. I support the charity Dignity In Dying, campaigning to change the law to allow the choice of an assisted death for terminally ill, mentally competent adults, within upfront safeguards. You can read more about it here: www.DignityInDying.org.uk

If you want to read more on the themes of this book

Bedlam: London and its mad – Catharine Arnold

The Locked Ward: Memoirs of a psychiatric orderly – Dennis O'Donnell

What is Madness? – Darian Leader

Mad, Bad and Sad: A history of women and the mind doctors from 1800 to the present – Lisa Appignanesi

Failed by the NHS – BBC documentary with Jonny Benjamin

Touched with Fire: Manic-depressive illness and the artistic temperament – Kay Redfield Jamison

(Life:) Razorblades Included – Dan Holloway

Poetry by Sylvia Plath and Anne Sexton

MORE BOOKS BY J.F.PENN

Thanks for joining Jamie and Blake in *Delirium*.

Sign up at www.JFPenn.com/free to be
notified of the next book in the series and
receive my monthly updates and giveaways.

* * *

Brooke and Daniel Psychological Thrillers

Desecration #1
Delirium #2
Deviance #3

* * *

Mapwalker Dark Fantasy Thrillers

Map of Shadows #1
Map of Plagues #2
Map of the Impossible #3

If you enjoy **Action Adventure Thrillers**, check out the
ARKANE series as Morgan Sierra and Jake Timber solve
supernatural mysteries around the world.

Stone of Fire #1
Crypt of Bone #2
Ark of Blood #3
One Day In Budapest #4
Day of the Vikings #5

Gates of Hell #6
One Day in New York #7
Destroyer of Worlds #8
End of Days #9
Valley of Dry Bones #10
Tree of Life #11

* * *

For more **dark fantasy,** check out:

Risen Gods
The Dark Queen
A Thousand Fiendish Angels:
Short stories based on Dante's Inferno

More books coming soon.

You can sign up to be notified of new releases, giveaways
and pre-release specials - plus, get a free book!

www.JFPenn.com/free

If you loved the book and have a moment to spare, I would
really appreciate a short review on the page where you
bought the book. Your help in spreading the word is grate-
fully appreciated and reviews make a huge difference to
helping new readers find the series.

Thank you!

ABOUT J.F.PENN

J.F.Penn is the Award-nominated, New York Times and USA Today bestselling author of the ARKANE action adventure thrillers, Brooke & Daniel Psychological Thrillers, and the Mapwalker fantasy adventure series, as well as other stand-alone stories.

Her books weave together ancient artifacts, relics of power, international locations and adventure with an edge of the supernatural. Joanna lives in Bath, England and enjoys a nice G&T.

You can follow Joanna's travels on Instagram @jfpennauthor and also on her podcast at BooksAndTravel.page.

* * *

Sign up for your free thriller,
Day of the Vikings, and updates from behind the scenes, research, and giveaways at:

www.jfpenn.com/free

* * *

Connect with Joanna:
www.JFPenn.com
joanna@JFPenn.com
www.Facebook.com/JFPennAuthor
www.Instagram.com/JFPennAuthor

* * *

For writers:

Joanna's site, www.TheCreativePenn.com, helps people write, publish and market their books through articles, audio, video and online courses.

She writes non-fiction for authors under Joanna Penn and has an award-nominated podcast for writers, The Creative Penn Podcast.

ACKNOWLEDGEMENTS

Thanks to Dan Holloway, for writing so eloquently on aspects of mental illness, for answering my questions and for being a superb beta-reader and helping me improve the story. And to Garry Rodgers, ex-coroner, for checking my death scenes.

Thanks to Jen Blood, my editor, for her fantastic work in improving the text, and to Wendy Janes for excellent proof-reading.

Thanks, as always, to Derek Murphy from Creativindie for the fantastic book cover design. And to Jane Dixon Smith for the interior design.

9 781913 321284